Dream Lover

Charle McDaniel

Ms.WRiTE
Publications

ISBN-13: 978-0-9848890-2-0

First Printing 2018

Cover design by C Ford

Published by:

Ms. Write Publications
Rockwall, TX 75087
charlemcdaniel.com

Published in the United States of America

This novel is dedicated to two of the most amazing women in my life

Tiffany Edwards
A true ray of sunshine in my world. Thank you, Tiffany,
for being my biggest cheerleader and for being such
an amazing friend.

and

Paula Bradley
A dear friend and fellow author. Thank you, Paula,
for being a gracious and hospitable source of knowledge,
and for offering such invaluable advice.

Also by Charle McDaniel

The Manicure

Blaze

Rustic Meadows

Code Blue

ACKNOWLEDGEMENTS

I would like to thank the following women for allowing me to bring their characters to life in my story.

Ducky (*Butch*), for being a loyal friend and an incredible character in real life.

Dawn (*Biff*), for your uncanny humor and literal way of stating the obvious.

Barbara (*Marge*), for always having the courage to be bold and adventurous.

and

A special thank you to Shane for filling my mind with notions of love and happiness. I am still hopeful that one day we will actually meet.

PROLOGUE

The human psyche is an amazing phenomenon in that its sole purpose is to engage, promote, protect and preserve its host. At times, however, the distinction between reality and fantasy may lose clarity. The mind tends to choose fact over fiction, but what if it can no longer tell the difference? Does that make it any less real?

—— CRIES FROM THE DARK ——

There was a time when my world was plagued by a series of daydreams, each filled with flashbacks of my life. They happened so often it felt like I was living in a perpetual state of confusion, grappling to ascertain what was then, what was now, and what was yet to come. The first one occurred while I was sitting in a booth at a diner. Being single, I rarely cooked for myself and the diner was close to my house, the food was good and the service exceptional, so it made perfect sense as to why I spent so much time there.

From the very start the dreams riveted me with haunting memories of days gone by and, like a fly caught in a spider's web, I became entangled in the lost days of my past. Oftentimes they were filled with images emerging from the depths of old memories, each with a voice of its own crying out and begging me to hold on. At times I longed to disappear with them, hoping to share their one-way venture into the dark hole from which they had appeared. Instead, I was trapped, imprisoned in a strange reality created by the characters that lived inside of those dreams.

Sometime back, long before the daydreams started, life was simpler and a hell of a lot happier. How long ago was that? I couldn't remember. Not that it mattered anymore. The life I knew seemed to have disappeared in the blink of an eye. There I was, alone again and miserable for the umpteenth time in my thirty-five years.

I couldn't control when the daydreams would occur and had more or less come to terms with that. I could, however, tell when one was about to commence. Each time, it felt like the walls of the diner were closing in around me. I tried willing them to stop, but the walls, deaf and apathetic, continued to advance.

Occasionally my requests were granted momentary reprieves but the victory didn't last. The reverie would always take over and command their movement once again. I knew the ritual well for all too often it came; same dark setting, same cast of characters. Under the dream's spell, my consciousness would plunge into submission and I was powerless to stop it.

—— Mama Loves You ——

The daydreams seemed to build off of one another, each new one picking up where the last one left off. It all began with a young girl clinging to the hem of an older woman's skirt.

"Who are you?" I asked the girl. "Why do you look so familiar? Do I know you?"

She didn't answer. The look in her dark, round eyes told me she might be afraid to answer. That look offered a reflection into my own burdened soul.

I continued to scan her face for clues to her identity. We shared many of the same physical attributes: olive skin, brown hair and brown eyes. The bruises and marks on her arms were as noticeable as they had been on me when I was a child.

Don't be afraid, I wanted to tell her, but the words that formed in my brain stopped just shy of my lips. How could I, of all people, expect this timid creature to put her faith in the advice of a stranger? Would I have done so at her age?

My focus shifted to the woman, who appeared to be agitated by the youngster's incessant clinging.

"Let go of me," she snapped. Within seconds a false smile wormed its way across her mouth as she turned to face the girl. "It's only for a few months. Now quit acting like a baby. It'll be fun. You'll see."

She grabbed the child's arm and pushed her into a crowd of people waiting to board an airplane. The girl didn't cry or make a scene, perhaps knowing such an act would only upset the woman and trigger her rage.

It was at this stage of the dream that I realized I was the little girl and the woman was my mother. The first feelings of fear and repulsion then settled over me as the dream moved on to expose even more tragedies of my youth.

"Hurry up," my mother grated, her lips curled in a snarl as her face neared mine.

To anyone watching, the tall, raven-haired woman with charcoal eyes appeared to be sharing an intimate goodbye with her daughter. It was a command performance. She was quite masterful at disguising her true self in public. Everyone who met her thought she was the sweetest, most kind person on the planet. But I knew the truth. There was a villain lurking beneath that outer beauty.

"Get on up there. Go on now. That pilot isn't going to wait for the likes of you. I will never hear the end of it if your aunt and uncle are there to pick you up and you are not on that plane."

There I stood, surrounded by strangers, a skinny four-year-old with tear-stained cheeks and puffy circles under my eyes. There was a slump to my shoulders and sadness etched on my face, mixed with pain and bewilderment. Pain because of the bruises and marks on my arms, coupled with my mother's crushing grip having dragged me through the concourse (my suitcase pulled by her other hand); bewilderment because I assumed she was shipping me off for something bad I had done.

That was the first of many summer "trips" where I was sent to a family of relatives who agreed to surrogate on my mother's behalf. In the weeks that followed my arrival, I stayed on my best behavior in hopes of impressing those who had taken me in.

Maybe, I remembered thinking, *after summer is over, they'll tell my mother that I was a good girl and she won't send me away again. Maybe their words will warm her icy heart. Maybe…*

While standing in line I turned for one last look and raised my tiny hand in a feeble attempt at goodbye. My mother raised hers also and yelled out, "Bye, baby. You be good, you hear me? Mama loves you!"

In that dream I aged dramatically during flight and deplaned as a fifteen-year-old, the same age that I spent my final summer away from home. Instead of being welcomed into the arms of relatives I was greeted by a man, an intentional date arranged by my mother, a woman overly concerned by the fact that her only daughter, now on the cusp of womanhood, still hadn't shown the slightest interest in the opposite sex.

I tried to force myself awake at that point with clenched fists and fingernails dug deep into my palms, but the dream continued. The teenage girl emerged from the recesses of the darkness and placed a clock and a calendar on the table before me. The hands on the clock began to spin counterclockwise, slowly at first then faster as the hours passed. Corresponding pages of the calendar peeled away, month after month, year after year. Both stopped when the date reached April 6, 1965.

The dream then transformed into a voyeuristic journey, playing like a movie screen in my mind. Through closed eyes I saw the living room that I played in as a child being brought into focus.

In 1965 I spent most of my time indoors watching television during the wet rainy days of spring, and that particular day in April was no different. As I sat cross-legged on the living room floor, I could hear my mother calling me from the kitchen. It was crazy to think I could get away with ignoring her, but, at five I didn't know any better so I did it anyway, hoping to buy time until the next commercial break. Not my best plan.

"Damn it, Dusty!" she yelled as she stormed into the room, stopping in front of the screen to deliberately block my view. "Didn't you hear me calling you?"

"No, ma'am," I answered softly.

The tone of her voice told me I was going to pay dearly for that lapse in judgment. Afraid to look in her direction, I kept my head lowered.

She lunged forward and grabbed a handful of my hair, lifting me at least six or seven inches off of the floor. I was a scrawny kid, small for my age, so it didn't take much for her to overpower me. Because of my size, most people treated me like a fragile, china doll. My mother was not one of those people.

"I know you heard me, you lying little bitch," she hissed, her black eyes staring into mine. "When I call, you had better answer. Do you understand me?"

"Yes, ma'am," I sobbed, sniffling as my fingers groped for her hands, desperate to pry them from my hair. "I won't do it again, I promise. Please let go! You're hurting me!"

"Stop that crying. If you don't stop, I will really give you something to cry about!"

But I couldn't stop. The pain was too intense. True to her word, she dragged me to the kitchen, pulled a wooden spoon from a drawer and beat me across the ass with it. Afterwards, she shoved me to the floor and ordered me to get out of her face.

I shuffled back to the living room on my knees while holding my burning cheeks in both hands. Occasionally I touched my head to check for signs of bleeding. Through it all, my whimpering continued.

"Shut up!" she screamed. "Stop that goddamn noise! If you don't stop that crying this instant, I swear to God, I will knock you into next week!"

Marching into the room again she raised her hand to slap me. I instinctively lifted my arms as a shield. It wasn't the first time that I had needed to defend myself, and, even at that tender age, I was fully aware it wouldn't be the last time either.

"If I had never met your father, you wouldn't be here," she said as she backhanded me across the face.

That was an expression I heard so many times that even I wished she had never met my father. They were married less than thirty days when she got knocked up. After learning she was pregnant, he denied paternity, accusing her of whoring around while he was at work. One night, in a drunken fury, he punched her in the stomach, determined to terminate the bastard seed he believed was growing inside of her. Eventually he passed out and she escaped with her life – and mine. Bloodied and battered she hailed a passerby, a Good Samaritan who bought a one-way bus ticket for her to return to her family.

With help from her parents the marriage ended in divorce and she was rid of him forever. Unfortunately, his image would continue to haunt her because I look exactly like the man she had come to despise.

—— I'M NOT LIKE OTHER GIRLS ——

I visited the diner so often that I had become well acquainted with the entire staff. Mabel, the daytime waitress, was my favorite. An older woman in her sixties, she treated me as though I were one of her own children. Her concern for me was genuine and I was truly grateful.

As I sat in the booth that day my body began to recoil from the abuse the same as it had that rainy April in 1965. Mabel, out of concern or sympathy, came to stand beside me and placed her hand on my shoulder. Giving it a little squeeze, she asked, "Are you all right?"

Upon her touch, the dream released its grip long enough for me to answer.

"I'm okay. Thanks. Could I get another glass of water?"

No sooner than she was gone, the dream resumed. The hands on the clock began to move once more, this time in a forward direction. Pages from the calendar reapplied themselves until coming to a stop on

September 26, 1966. The movie started again with me as a six-year-old standing in the middle of the playground at my elementary school.

I had my first crush when I was six. The object of my pre-pubescent desire was a classmate named Celeste. Though there were several young ladies worthy of my attention at Fulton Elementary, my heart belonged to Celeste. All eyes were drawn to the blue-eyed, petite girl with pale, pink skin and platinum blond hair. Every girl longed to be her friend, while boys with even the slightest bit of testosterone vied to win her fancy. For me, it was easier to associate with the latter. Even teachers and school officials could be overheard commenting on how beautiful she was.

It was the third week of school when Celeste first approached me and introduced herself. She was wearing a colorful, lace-trimmed dress with yellow socks and black patent leather shoes that day, her blond hair parted down the middle and pulled into ponytails that jutted out from either side of her head just above the ear. I looked like a country bumpkin in comparison with my green sundress and brown saddle oxfords, uneven bangs (the unfortunate result of a chewing gum bubble that went awry), and a huge black hole where my two front teeth had once been.

My first words to her were nothing more than a bunch of garbled sounds. As the conversation continued my shyness waned and I was able to contribute on a more equal basis, which was a big deal considering I rarely ever said more than a few words to anyone. Not even at home. I usually only socialized through sports.

Because of her outgoing personality, Celeste was the most popular girl in all of first grade and swarms of kids were always following her around. After meeting her I began to tag along as well, but always a step or two behind the pack.

Being naturally athletic I was routinely chosen when team selections were made for playground games. Only a handful of girls were good enough to play alongside the boys and I was always first pick from that bunch. Those not chosen, including Celeste, would watch from the sidelines. And although her attention to me was indirect, it felt good knowing she was there.

One bright, sun-filled day in October, Celeste and I, along with a handful of others, were walking past a group of kids forming teams for dodgeball when, all of a sudden, she reached out and grabbed my arm. That simple touch stirred feelings in me that I wouldn't understand for many years to come.

"Look!" she shrieked. "Dodgeball! I love dodgeball!"

"Let's go play!" I replied excitedly.

"I can't. My mom will tan my hide if I get this dress dirty. You go ahead."

"I can play dodgeball anytime. I would rather stay here with you."

Though pleased with my decision, my shoulders sagged with disappointment. It wasn't like me to turn down a game of dodgeball, or any other game for that matter.

"I like hanging out with you," Celeste confided. "You're my best friend, Dusty."

"Mine, too," I answered, then expressed silently, *You're my* only *friend*.

From that day forward I followed her like a puppy on a leash. If she stopped at the water fountain, I stood behind her until she was finished. If she went to the restroom, I waited for her in the hall. The only time we were separated was at recess when she stayed behind with the other girls while I ventured off to play with the boys.

By midyear, most of the kids in school were referring to me as "one of the guys." I always knew I wasn't like the other girls so it didn't really bother me. Honestly, it felt quite normal. I'm sure I was already identifying as a lesbian but wasn't old enough yet to put that kind of label on it.

My mother never participated in sports and hated the fact that I did. She remarried when I was a year old and "Pop," the nickname I gave my stepfather, would go against her wishes by encouraging me to play and would rile her even further by occasionally coming to my games. He had a quiet passion for athletics and I think I reminded him of a younger, female version of himself.

To my mother, my tomboyish ways were unacceptable.

"I don't know why I bother trying to make you look pretty," she complained. "Look at you. Your hair is a mess, your clothes are filthy and your shoes are all scuffed up. Young ladies are supposed to be refined, not ruffians."

By her standards, I was in constant violation of the rules of etiquette required for proper young ladies, a crime that was punishable by grounding. Needless to say, I spent a great majority of my adolescence confined to my room.

- - - - - - - - - - - - - - - - - - - -

My crush on Celeste continued for several years. A few days before the end of fourth grade she told me that her father had accepted a job in another state and that they would be moving away before the start of the next school year. I was shattered. To add to my despair, one week later my mother packed my bags and shipped me off to Oklahoma to spend the summer with my Aunt Helen and her family. I knew that Celeste would be gone before I returned.

Helen was my favorite aunt but had little to offer in the way of consolation. I cried every day over the loss of my friend. It was an unbearably long, traumatic summer.

The start of fifth grade brought together the same old faces as well as some new ones. Jennifer, one of two new girls in class, had moved to town from Cedar Rapids, Iowa. Sharon, the other, hailed from Wisconsin. I'd been to Iowa a few times and thought it was a bore. Wisconsin, however, was a place I had only read about in books. That gave Sharon an immediate one-up on Jennifer.

Jennifer was a loner, very quiet and reserved. I said "hello" a few times but never got anything out of her. Sharon, on the other hand, was extremely extroverted and would talk your ear off. She was fun and upbeat, always making people laugh. I liked her a lot. She seemed to like me as well and it wasn't long before she began to fill Celeste's void.

Sharon and I did most things together, a tradition that carried on into our teens. On the rare times I wasn't grounded we would hang out with the "cool" chicks, the girls who smoked and drank and chased boys. Well, they chased boys. I just smoked and drank. A lot (of both). In fact, my initiation into the group was on my eleventh birthday when they all pitched in to buy me a carton of cigarettes. It was clear that if I was going to be *in* with them, I had to be *one* of them. As teenagers we were a fairly rowdy bunch and did some pretty stupid things, most of which got me in trouble at home, too.

Sharon was a few months older than me and got her driver's license before I did. She taught me how to drive her dad's pickup in the parking lot of our high school. She was the only person I shared everything with, including the truth about my mother. While she couldn't save me from the troubles I had at home, she did manage to get me out of the house every once in a while. Whenever possible we would sneak off to the drive-in movies, a bottle of Sloe Gin (purchased by one of the older kids in town) and a six-pack of 7-Up stashed under a blanket on the floorboard of that old pickup. Every time I got a drink or two under my belt I would start to cry. Sharon had no advice to offer, no words of wisdom to make anything better, but she did provide a safe place to escape, albeit temporarily, life with my parents. I'm not sure I would have survived those years had it not been for her.

By age fourteen, I was drinking every weekend. The only change in my routine was the person who shared my booze. Most times it was Sharon, but when she couldn't make it, I had no problem finding someone else to take her place. It was a small town. There really wasn't anything else to do. Except chase boys.

My girlfriends were crazy about boys. One even got pregnant while I was away for the summer and ended up having an abortion. Me? Not so much. I had boy "friends" from school, but they were no more than teammates on the sports field. There were plenty of suitors, all of which I politely refused. It seemed the more dates I turned away, the more estranged I became from my friends and my parents. I wanted to fit in but found the whole dating scene repulsive. Everyone knew I was different, but no one, including myself, knew what that difference was or what it meant. Homosexuality didn't exist in our small town. Or if it did, it was buried deep inside someone's closet.

When I turned fifteen, my mother, now more determined than ever to mold me into a "real" daughter, began choosing my clothes, my hairstyles and even my friends on her mission to make me more feminine. Blue jeans had become the norm in 1975, but I was still forced to wear a dress or skirt every day to school. It was humiliating.

"You are my daughter," she said, her voice rumbling like the Lord God Almighty's. "You will not leave this house dressed like those damn freak hippies down the street."

"Pop wears jeans every day," I countered. "He doesn't look like a hippie."

"Your father is a grown man and can wear what he wants. I have no control over that. You, on the other hand, will do as I say. I will skin you alive if I ever catch you in a pair of jeans. Do you hear me?"

I glared at her but said nothing.

"*Do you hear me?*" she asked again.

"Yes, ma'am. I heard you."

"All right then. Now go put on that new skirt I bought for you last week."

That skirt isn't new, I argued silently. *You picked it up at a garage sale just like that putrid dress last month. Oh, didn't I tell you? That went over well when Betty Allen saw me wearing her old clothes. I was the brunt of her jokes for the entire day.*

"Don't just stand there. Go get dressed or you'll be late for school. They're taking pictures today, aren't they? I think you should wear that white top with the lace collar. It will go perfect with that skirt."

"I am not a child," I mumbled as I turned to leave. "I'm fifteen, for Christ's sake."

Before my foot hit the floor, she grabbed my arm and spun me around.

"What did you say?"

"I didn't say anything."

"Don't you sass me, girl. I will slap that shit right out of you."

"Yes, ma'am."

"Are you sassing me now?" she asked, confused by my answer.

"No, ma'am. I'm not sassing you." *Not out loud, anyway.*

I turned on my heels and marched up the stairs, angry that my voice had once again been silenced when it came to picking my own wardrobe. I begrudgingly put on the skirt and blouse and, with barely enough time to win her approval, raced out the front door.

I was the only student in line for photographs that day not wearing denim, making me an obvious outcast amongst my peers. It was one of the darkest days of my life. The picture in the yearbook clearly captured my mood: sad, somber, drawn and defeated.

- -

My mother's attitude worsened over time. In her opinion, voiced to anyone within earshot, I would never amount to anything since I lacked the cleaning, cooking and sewing skills necessary to make anyone, particularly my future husband, happy. Her comments were hurtful and I found it necessary to prove I was a good person in spite of her noted shortcomings. It was important (for some insane reason I will never understand) that she take pride in my accomplishments. I consistently performed above and beyond other students in academics, music and sports and received tons of kudos from teachers and coaches. But there was never one compliment or congratulation from my mother.

That summer, I was sent back to Oklahoma. Fortunately, shipping me off to Aunt Helen's that year was the best thing my mother ever did for me. Not only was Helen a positive, loving role model, she also gave me insight into what my mother was like as a young girl. Our stories were the same. My mother wasn't any nicer to Helen than she had been to me. Not a big shocker there.

"I'm afraid of her," I confessed reluctantly, visibly embarrassed and saddened by my admission.

"You're giving her your power," Helen replied. "Take it back. Don't disrespect her; she is still your mother. But don't let her change who you are. You're special, Dusty. One of a kind. And you're beautiful. Don't let her convince you otherwise."

She smiled at me before continuing.

"I was afraid of her when I was a kid, too. One day, I think I was your age or maybe a little younger, your grandmother caught her bossing me around and told me to stop being a doormat and stand up for myself. I did, and your mother hasn't bothered me since.

"You're going to have to do the same thing, princess. She has pushed you and your father around for all these years. He is going to push back one of these days. So will you."

I never gave much thought to the fact that my stepfather might also be a victim of my mother's verbal assaults. He was a soft-spoken man who spent most of his time on projects that kept him away from the house. That must have made life more tolerable for him. I wish I had that option. In dealing with my mother, I sensed that he and I were a lot alike. Since standing up for ourselves only served to fuel her quest for control, we held our tongues instead. I bottled up my hatred, resentment and anger on the inside. I'm sure he did the same as well.

I loved my stepfather and truly believed that he loved me, too. Most people thought we looked just alike, which we both found incredibly funny since we didn't share a single ounce of DNA.

Pop was ten when his father was killed in the war. At thirteen, he started working to help provide for his mother and younger sister, which robbed him of his childhood. He likely encouraged me to play sports because it gave him an opportunity to experience those things vicariously through me.

—— Auld Lang Syne ——

Several days passed before the next daydream occurred. This one hurried through my adolescence very quickly as the pages on the calendar and hands on the clock raced to keep time. Both came to an abrupt halt at the stroke of midnight on December 31, 1976. The movie started immediately after, opening with me and my mother standing together in an uncomfortable embrace.

My stepfather never said anything about my mother, good or bad, which, despite all of their arguing, made me believe they had a strong marriage. On New Year's Eve, 1976, they went out with friends to celebrate what was to be their last night together as a couple. At midnight, Pop gathered everyone around and announced that he was divorcing my mother. It was a premeditated plan to annihilate her in front of their friends, perhaps in retaliation for the many times she had ambushed him in similar fashion. She was caught off guard and came home alone, justifiably devastated.

When I learned what had happened, I was overwhelmed by my stepfather's cruelty and felt sorry for her. Granted, my mother wasn't the nicest person on Earth, but he didn't have to destroy her like that in front of their friends. She was that way because… Well, because that's who she was. But not Pop. His was an act of deliberate cruelty. I had always thought of him as a decent, kind and respectful man. His behavior that night devastated me as well and my opinion of him was forever changed.

My mother needed consolation, as did I, but neither of us knew how so we managed an awkward hug before she excused herself to make phone calls to her family. I went to my bedroom and shut the door.

Over the next two weeks a plan was hatched to move my mother and me to Texas to be near her relatives. I was not privy to that arrangement and only learned of it the day I came home from school and found a U-

Haul truck parked in our front yard, fully loaded, engine running. Pop was leaning against the bumper smoking a cigarette.

"What's going on?" I asked as I came closer.

"You and your mother are going to Texas."

"For how long?"

"You're moving there."

"What? Why?"

"We decided it would be best for everyone."

"No one asked me! I don't want to move to Texas. And I don't want to go with *her*. Why can't I stay here with you?"

I wanted him to fight for me, but he wasn't having any part of it.

"You're going with your mom," he said. "She's your blood and you belong with her."

His words cut like a knife. Blood had never played a part in our relationship before. Why did it suddenly matter now?

I ran past him into the house and made several frantic calls to friends in hopes that one could help me find a way to stay in Missouri. I didn't want to leave. This was my home. This was where I belonged.

Sharon came over right away and together we pleaded with my parents to let me stay behind. Both refused. Less than twenty minutes later, my mother and I were on the road to Texas. There was nothing I could do but sit in silent agony and watch the only world I had ever known or cared about disappear behind us.

Once again, I felt betrayed by the very two people who were supposed to love me. I wanted to cry or scream out, but couldn't. I was gutted, empty of emotion. It felt like my heart had been ripped from my chest and a large, gaping hole left in its wake. A new "me" was borne in that moment and a tough, impenetrable wall went up to prevent either of them from ever hurting me again.

With my sense of trust completely destroyed, I withdrew to a place deep inside; a place where I felt safe from the world. I vowed to stay in that place forever to protect and preserve what was left of me.

—— DEEP IN THE HEART OF TEXAS ——

I celebrated my seventeenth birthday two weeks after arriving in Texas. It wasn't much of a celebration. My grandmother and I spent the entire day unpacking boxes. No one from Missouri, not even Pop, now living with his girlfriend, phoned in with birthday wishes, making the day even more of a downer.

Out of sight, out of mind, I thought with a morbid sense of resolve. *No biggie. I can get by just fine without those people. Who needs them anyway? Not me.*

As I wallowed in self-pity, my grandmother handed me a small, wrapped present.

"Happy birthday, sweetheart," she said with a smile. "This is probably the worst birthday ever, isn't it?"

I nodded slowly, fighting back tears. She reached out to touch my cheek, catching a stray droplet that had managed to elude my tough facade.

"I know this isn't where you want to be, but I'm glad you're here."

"Thanks, Gram."

"This has been hard on your mom, you know, but she is doing what is best for you. You're all that matters to her now."

That's a scary thought, I shuddered.

My grandmother was a kind, gentle soul. Oddly, my mother did not inherit any of those traits. She was more like her father, a militant man who often treated his children as though they were his subordinates rather than his own flesh and blood.

We were now living with my grandmother in the same house my mother grew up in. Not much had changed in all of the years since. Wood panels still dressed the walls throughout the interior, making everything appear dark and dreary. The bedroom floors were covered in the original shag carpet, worn nearly bare at the entrance to each room. In the kitchen was an old assortment of avocado-colored appliances, all working as good as when they were brand new.

Our house was four blocks from the high school that my mother attended in her youth. Her allegiance to her alma mater was unmoving and I was enrolled within days of our arrival.

The new school was much larger than the one in Missouri, with kids constantly bustling through its corridors. I walked the halls for the first half of the day, unable to find any of the classrooms that were listed on my schedule. As luck would have it, a very pretty girl in a faded, denim jacket and cowboy boots came to my rescue.

"You look lost," she said, tilting her head slightly. "Need some help?"

"That would be great. I'm looking for Band class."

"I'm in that class. I can show you where it is. Come on. Follow me."

We passed by the cafeteria and turned right down one hallway, left down another then right down one more.

"Here we are," she said as we rounded the last corner.

"They need to put a map in the Welcome Kit," I said half-jokingly. "I never would have found this place on my own."

She looked at me and smiled.

"How many classes have you missed today?"

"All of them. I found one five minutes after the bell rang but didn't go in."

"So, what have you been doing all morning?"

"Hanging out in the restroom, mostly."

"You must be a smoker."

"Why do you say that?"

"All the new kids go in there to light up."

"Oh. Do you smoke?"

"Yeah, but not in there. The campus cops will bust you if they catch you smoking in the bathroom. We go behind the school during lunch break. If you want, I can take you there after class."

"That would be awesome. Thanks."

"What's your name?"

"Dusty."

"I'm Alison. Nice to meet you, Dusty."

"Nice to meet you, too."

She pushed the door open and led me to the instructor who quickly paired me with an old horn from the property room. I joined a small group of saxophone players while Alison retreated to the drum section.

Poised over a trap set with her sticks tapping on the snare, she maintained a steady beat for the rest of us to follow. Halfway through the song she broke out into a solo that caused everyone to stop and take notice. A big smile spread across my face as I watched her body moving to the rhythm of her own cadence.

Wow, I mused. *Not only is this girl attractive, she is amazingly talented, too.*

Alison must have found me equally impressive because I caught her staring at me several times throughout the rehearsal. I moved my music stand to try and block her view, but there were so many percussion instruments that she would simply switch from one to another to clear her sights and focus on me again. I was frightened and flattered at the same time. I had never met anyone like her and didn't know what to make of it.

After class, I followed her to the smoker's hangout where a handful of kids were already puffing away.

"Hey, Al," one of the boys said as we snaked our way into the crowded space.

"Hi, Bobby," came her reply.

"Who's your friend?"

"This is Dusty. She just moved here from..."

Lost for an answer, Alison turned to me. Her light brown hair was shag cut to frame her face, drawing attention to the most sparkling pair of emerald green eyes I had ever seen. I was immediately transfixed.

"Does she speak?" Bobby asked, breaking my spell.

"Yes," I muttered shyly. "I'm from Missouri."

Unimpressed with my response, he turned his back to us. Alison and I now had the opportunity to speak freely and privately.

"See?" she said, smiling. "I told you. No cops out here."

"Aren't we still on school grounds?"

"Yeah, but they won't come outside."

"Why not?"

"Too busy watching everyone in the cafeteria, I guess."

Leaning against the wall, Alison reached into her pocket and pulled out a pack of Marlboros. She tapped the pack on the back of her hand and two cigarettes surfaced. She pulled them out together and handed one to me.

"So, when did you move here?"

"A couple weeks ago."

"And you're from Missouri? I've never been there. What's it like?"

"Mostly farm country. Lots of corn. And cows."

"I'm not a fan of cows. There's a statue of a longhorn in front of the western store where I got my boots. That's as close as it gets for me."

Her offhanded remark made me laugh and she soon joined in as well. Our small talk continued until the bell rang and forced our conversation to an end. She then walked me to my next class, promising to join up with me again the following day.

- -

Alison and I continued meeting in "The Lounge" (as the smokers called it) over the next few days, every meeting adding more substance to our budding friendship. It was at one of those outings that she asked about my parents.

"Not much to tell," I said. It was an outright fib, but she didn't need to know that. Not yet, anyway.

"You never talk about them, only your grandmother. I figured you were orphaned or something."

"No. I live with my mom at my grandmother's house. My dad stayed in Missouri."

"My folks have been married for thirty-seven years."

"Damn. They must be pretty old."

"They are. I have an older brother and two older sisters. I was an oops baby. My youngest sister is ten years older than me."

"I don't have any brothers or sisters."

"You're lucky. They can be a real pain in the ass sometimes."

Our chatter ended abruptly with the clanging of the school bell.

"Where do you live?" she asked as we headed back inside.

Pointing over my shoulder, I responded, "Four blocks that way."

"I live that way, too. Why don't we walk home together?"

"I'd like that."

"Okay. Let's meet here after school. I'll catch you later!"

Fortunately, the rest of the day passed quickly and when the final bell rang, I bolted from class, racing toward The Lounge at top speed as I zig-zagged past other students in the hall.

Out of my way, people! Move it! Come on, folks. Get the hell out of the way!

My heart was fluttering with excitement and anticipation.

I am walking home with Alison, I thought cheerfully, bragging mutely to everyone in my path. *How cool is that?*

We arrived at the same time and started across the parking lot together. Our first few steps were shrouded with silence, but by the time we reached the main road we were talking over one another. As we neared Alison's street, she lagged behind for a moment and then sped past me.

"My mom teaches Spanish at St. Mary's," she said, stopping quickly and turning on her heels. "She gets home before everyone else so she's probably there if you want to come in and say hello."

I agreed and followed her the half-block to her house. She opened the front door and a small, wirehaired dog ran out onto the stoop to greet her.

"Max," she scolded, pushing the dog aside. "Get down."

"Awww... How cute!"

"Don't let the cuteness fool you. He's a nuisance."

The dog, realizing his needs weren't getting met, turned his attention to me.

"Mamacita!" Alison yelled out. "Are you home?"

"Yes, mija," a small voice answered back. "I'm in the kitchen."

"I have someone with me."

"Please tell me you didn't bring home another stray."

"Kind of," Alison chuckled, elbowing my ribs. "But it's a stray girl this time."

Her mother entered the room and I saw right away where Alison's green eyes came from. "Hello," she said, extending her hand. My arm was nearly shaken out of its socket as I uttered a meek "Hey" in response.

Still clutching my hand, she asked, "What is your name?" and finally let go when I answered, "My name is Dusty."

Her eyes then shifted to her daughter.

"Alison, are you and your friend hungry? I'm making enchiladas."

"She is standing right here, Mom. Why don't you ask her yourself?"

The tiny framed woman gave her a disappointing glare before turning back to me.

"Would you like to stay for dinner, Dusty? I can call your parents if you want."

"My mother doesn't get off until seven," I lied, knowing full well the she-devil was already at home. "Besides, she won't care if I stay."

That was another lie. I knew I would get my ass whipped if I wasn't home by 5:30. Still, it was a risk I was willing to take.

Alison's father, also a teacher, joined us in the kitchen a short while later. After a quick introduction he grabbed a handful of plates and passed them to his daughter.

"Go set the table," he said. He then snatched a handful of silverware from an open drawer and handed those to me. "Here. Since you're staying, you have to help out, too."

"Alberto," his wife chided.

"I don't mind," I responded, grinning.

The talk around the dinner table was entertaining, everyone sharing details of their day as serving dishes were passed from person to person. I sat quietly and listened. At one point, Alison prodded me to join the conversation.

"Feel free to jump in anytime," she urged with a jabbed finger into my side.

"She might not be comfortable with that," her father objected. He then turned to me and offered, "You don't have to say anything if you don't want to, Dusty."

His pardon unknowingly spared me a great deal of embarrassment as my shyness would never have allowed me to participate in that kind of banter. I returned his gaze with a smile of relief.

Alison leaned in close to me and whispered "chicken" under her breath.

Soundlessly, I countered, *You wouldn't call me 'chicken' if you knew what was waiting for me at home...*

"When is the spring concert?" Alison's mother asked, forcing a change of subject.

"Next Thursday," Alison responded. "You guys are coming, right?"

"Of course," her father answered.

"Dusty is in the band, too," Alison added. "She plays tenor sax."

"Our oldest daughter plays saxophone..."

"Alison has a big solo," her mother said, cutting him off. "What about you, Dusty? Are you playing any solo parts?"

"No, ma'am," I answered quietly. "I'm not that good."

"Yes, you are," Alison objected. "You wouldn't have gotten to be first chair if you weren't!"

Turning her head, she coughed out "chicken" once more.

"Alison!" her mother snapped. "Be nice."

I glanced at the clock on the wall and saw that it was nearly seven o'clock. I knew I would get the beating of my life if I stayed much longer.

"I should get going," I said, rising to my feet. "My mom should be home by now. Thank you very much for dinner."

"You're welcome," Alison's parents chimed together.

Alison's father handed her his keys and said, "Give Dusty a ride home. The sun will be going down soon and I don't want her out there alone in the dark."

"Sure thing, Papi. She doesn't live far so I shouldn't be gone very long."

Alison's mother draped her arm over my shoulder and ushered us to the front door.

"It was very nice meeting you, Dusty," she said. "Come again, anytime."

"Thank you, ma'am. I would like that very much."

She waited on the porch until the car pulled out of the driveway. It was then Alison turned to me and said, "You should really think about doing a solo."

"Are you nuts? I can't stand up and play in front of people like that!"

"Sure, you can. You have the talent. All you need are some cojones."

"What are cojones?"

"Balls. You know, for girls."

"And how do you propose I get some of those?"

"Stay overnight with me on Friday."

"What? How will staying over…"

"My family plays professionally and we have a gig at the Mexican Market. You can come and play with us if you want."

"I don't know about that."

"Why not? Come on, Dusty. Don't be a chicken your whole life. Jump out there. I won't let you fall."

I continued to contemplate her proposition as she pulled the car to a stop in front of my house.

"Want me to walk you to the door?" she asked.

"Nah, I'll be all right. Tell your folks thanks for me."

"Okay. See you at school tomorrow."

I opened the front door and stepped across the threshold slowly, unsure of what awaited me on the other side. My mother was standing just behind the door, far enough back that I couldn't see her.

"Where in the hell have you been?" she spouted loudly.

"A classmate asked me to dinner," I answered, startled by her sudden appearance. "I didn't think you would mind."

"Why would you think that? Of course I mind!"

She glared at me for some time before continuing.

"And just who is this classmate?"

"Her name is Alison. I met her in Band."

"Next time, young lady, you had better ask permission. I was worried sick!"

"I'm sorry. I didn't mean to upset you."

As I walked past, she reached out and whacked me on the back of the head.

"Go to your room this instant," she snarled. "And don't come out until morning."

I was a jumble of nerves that night, more from Alison's invitation to stay over than the fear of my mother's wrath. At breakfast the next morning I blurted out that I planned to spend the night at Alison's on Friday, given that it met with the she-devil's approval.

Gram was pleased that I had made a friend so soon and said "yes" right away. My mother, however, wanted to confirm it with Alison's parents before consenting. I dialed the number and handed her the phone before she even had time to finish her argument. A brief chat ensued, followed by an unbearable silence. I literally held my breath until she spoke again.

"All right. You can go as long as you finish your chores beforehand."

That was too easy. There had to be a catch in there somewhere. No matter. I would willingly take on whatever challenge she dished out. No chore was going to keep me from being with my new friend.

- - - - - - - - - - - - - - - - - - - -

Friday couldn't come fast enough. When it finally did, the hours at school seemed to drag on endlessly. I hurried home afterwards to find that my mother had a list of eight chores, all of which needed to pass her inspection before I was allowed to leave the house. I hurried through the first seven, winning approval for each one without much contention.

The last chore on the list was to clean the windows in my grandmother's sun room. I'm sure this one was added just so she could maintain control, assuming that I would not finish in time to go with Alison.

That particular room had five large window panels, each one consisting of 15 to 20 small slats of glass that opened and closed with the turn of a handle at the bottom of the sill. I knew it would be a challenge to clean them all, so I doggedly set to the task and was nearly finished with the last panel when Alison arrived to claim me.

My mother chose that very moment to complain that the windows weren't clean enough and refused to let me leave until it was done to her satisfaction. Alison offered to help in order to hurry things along but the she-devil rejected her offer, saying it was my chore and insisting that I do it alone. I argued that it made more sense to have two people versus one, to which my mother responded with a raised hand to my face.

We stared each other down for a few seconds and then I did something I never had the courage to do before. I stood up to her.

Jaws clenched, I raised my hand to hers and growled, "If you hit me one more time, I swear you will never see me again."

Her eyes fixed on mine as she slowly lowered her hand to her side. I stepped past her with my hand still raised and followed Alison out the front door. I wasn't sure what consequences my actions would have, but at that moment, I didn't care. Those windows were clean. She and I both knew it. I did everything she asked of me and there was no way in hell I was going to let her cheat me out of our deal.

In the car, Alison tried to bring up what had happened but I was too embarrassed and ashamed to talk about it. She respectfully let the subject drop and began discussing the night's performance instead.

An hour later I was alongside her family as they took to the stage. One by one they claimed their instruments: dad with his six-string flat top, mom and her bass, brother on the trumpet, one sister on tenor sax and the other on tambourine, and Alison on drums. The saxophone sister had brought along a second horn at Allison's request, and I managed to sneak onstage with it after the applause subsided, hiding, more or less, behind her. It was my first time hearing Mexican music but I played along fairly well, considering.

Back at her house, Alison laughed and joked about how nervous I looked.

"Your lips were blue," she giggled. "I have never seen anyone so scared."

"Yeah, well. You've been doing this your whole life."

"I know. I just thought it was cute. That's all I meant."

She fell onto the twin-sized mattress and scooted against the wall to make room for me. I laid on the edge of the bed, one foot on top of the covers, the other planted firmly on the floor. This was uncharted territory. I had never shared a bed with another human being before.

Alison reached across my torso to switch off the lamp. Moonlight peering through a window on an adjacent wall immediately replaced the dark, creating a spotlight across the length of the bed. She looked at me and smiled, causing my heart to plummet from my chest into my stomach.

"You okay?" she asked, her body still pressed against mine.

"Yeah. Sure. You?" I answered in breathy, staccato pants.

"I'm good. Tired, but good. Thanks for coming tonight. It was fun."

She rolled onto her side and closed her eyes. Within minutes, she was fast asleep. I stared at the ceiling for quite some time before my eyes closed as well.

I attended many Friday night performances after that, more for the fact of staying over than for playing with the band. On Saturday mornings Alison's mother would teach me Spanish as that was the language they primarily spoke at home. I tried hard to mimic her words, but my mangled pronunciation only caused her to laugh, almost to the point of hysteria. When Alison was in the room, she would call me "carnicero," which, I was told after much begging, translates to "butcher" in English.

I enjoyed being around Alison's family and was fast becoming one of them. The more time I spent in their company, the more my confidence (and cojones) grew. Not only in music, but in other areas of my life as well. I wasn't the same shy girl that had arrived from the Midwest a few months earlier. My newfound independence gave me the courage to start refusing the demands of my mother, each act of resistance causing new tensions between us. No longer able to control me or my actions, the she-devil boxed up my stuff and kicked me out two weeks before the school year ended.

—— FREE AT LAST ——

Alison was with me on my first day of freedom. It all began enthusiastically but soon withered as we discovered the huge gap between the part-time wages I made as a weekend checker at the corner drug store and anticipated living expenses. Though I had socked away most of the money I made babysitting and doing odd jobs for my neighbors in Missouri, it was clear that, at the tender age of seventeen,

I had not yet amassed my life's fortune. Finding an affordable place to live wasn't going to be easy.

Five grueling hours into the hunt we stumbled onto a duplex that was in my price range. The tiny unit had four rooms: a shoebox sized living room, a bedroom that could have easily passed for a closet, a microscopic kitchen and a bathroom so small you could literally sit on the toilet, wash your hands in the sink and wet your feet in the tub without ever having to move. Spacious, it was not. Total square footage couldn't have been more than 300 feet, maximum. But, at seventy-five dollars a month it was a steal.

Our next challenge was to find furnishings. Since the bedroom would barely fit an infant's crib, it was going to be tough finding anything that wouldn't monopolize the entire space. Luckily for me the Goodwill Store had just what I needed, a futon couch that folded out flat and could easily serve as sofa and bed. With its bright red, fake leather upholstery it wasn't pretty, but most things that cheap usually aren't. We must have looked like long lost members of the Beverly Hillbillies driving around with that big red thing tied to the top of my Pinto station wagon, a rusty, old heap I had purchased just days earlier with a small loan from my grandmother.

A young woman was on the front lawn setting up for a yard sale when I pulled into the driveway. Seconds after shutting off the ignition, she began shouting in my direction.

"Hey!" she yelled. "Don't even think about dropping that piece of crap off here. We have enough junk to get rid of already!"

"No worries," I called back. "This 'piece of crap' belongs to me. I'm moving in next door."

Her lips mouthed the word "sorry" as Alison and I hoisted the beast down from the top of the car, nearly dropping it in the process. It was a challenge, but we finally managed to get it up the front stairs and into the living room, which, thank goodness, was just inside the door.

Later that evening, my new neighbors, Nancy, the woman in the yard, and Ken, her husband, brought over the remaining items from their sale. A peace offering, I think. I was now the proud owner of five odd-matched dinner plates, four spoons, one steak knife, two butter knives, six forks, three plastic mugs, one bowl and a toaster. A few days later, Alison's parents contributed a portable black-and-white television that perched proudly atop an empty milk crate I "borrowed" (forgive me) from the local supermarket. When Nancy said I needed more color, I "adopted" a few plants (forgive me again) from various homes around the neighborhood.

I had everything a young exile needed: a place, some stuff and friends to call my own. This corner of the world was mine. It no longer mattered what my mother thought of me. I was going to make it just fine without her. I soon realized I didn't need her – or anyone else – to survive.

- - - - - - - - - - - - - - - - - - - -

My high school graduation came and went without much pomp and circumstance. A few of my relatives, including my mother, came to watch me get my diploma, but it was Alison's family that cheered the loudest when I crossed the stage. I had to leave right after the ceremony to make it to work on time, arriving at the drug store still in full graduation regalia. That earned a few snickers from customers and coworkers alike.

By the end of my first month in the duplex I was working full-time as a cashier. I'm sure my boss made the offer out of pity because of my situation but, pride be damned, I was grateful. I needed a real job with a real paycheck in order to survive.

Alison came by nearly every day to check on me. One of her sisters lived only a few blocks away and her parents finally relented to our nonstop pleading and agreed to let her stay over on occasion knowing that she was close by. With absolutely no money left after paying bills there was little to do but spend our time together in front of the television. Most nights you would find us draped over one another after the programming day ended, fast asleep, the snowy screen showering a faint light over our intertwined bodies. We were still platonic at that time; however, the dynamics of our relationship would forever change before summer's end.

One stormy, Saturday night, we huddled together on the couch to watch the movie *Love Story*, and when the female lead was diagnosed with cancer, Alison started to cry. Having never learned how to comfort from either of my parents, I sat still as a statue and stared at the television, hoping that she would just dry up on her own.

A few minutes later, still sobbing, she stretched out across the length of the sofa and laid her head on my lap. She turned to look at me, her eyes wet with tears, and I gently brushed back the hair that had fallen onto her face. We stared at one another while dead air consumed the space between us. Eventually her focus returned to the television and I breathed a sigh of relief.

It wasn't long after that her hand began trailing up and down my thigh, the tips of her fingers flowing rhythmically between the hem of my shorts and my kneecap. My heart began to pound inside of my chest and I started taking air in shallow, raspy breaths. I felt very hot *and* very faint. I thought I was dying.

"Is this bothering you?" she asked.

"No," I replied, my voice crackling with anticipation.

She sat up and moved beside me.

"I want to kiss you," she stated confidently, then cocked her head slightly as if in afterthought, adding, "Would that be all right?"

My head bobbed up and down and side to side simultaneously.

Leaning her body against mine, our lips met and her tongue quickly made its way inside my mouth. Before long we were in the throes of teenage passion, pawing at each other's clothes, spurred on by the treasures we were sure to find underneath. Inexperience led to some difficulty on Alison's part, but I instinctively knew what to do to pleasure her.

Afterwards, she curled up in the crook of my arm.

"I love you," she murmured.

Flashbacks of my mother reciting those same three words before shipping me off as a child instantly filled my mind. I stiffened, body frozen while my eyes darted back and forth on the ceiling above us. I sat upright, grabbed the pack of Marlboros from the coffee table (an empty box with a towel draped over it) and tapped it against my wrist. Several cigarettes flew onto the floor at the same time. I picked up two of them, lit one and handed it to her then lit the other for myself. I left the remaining cigarettes where they had landed.

"Did you hear me?" she asked in a demanding tone that sounded eerily similar to my mother's. "I said I love you."

I drew in a lung full of smoke and let it out slowly.

"Yeah, I heard you."

"Well?"

"Well, what?"

"When someone says they love you, you're supposed to say it back."

I had never before said those words aloud and wasn't sure I could bring myself to do it now. Instead, I kept silent while staring at the glowing ember between my fingers.

"Come on," Alison prodded. "Say it."

"Say what?"

"Say that you love me."

Without taking my eyes off the cigarette, I mumbled, "I love you." And just as I had expected, they were hollow words that didn't resound with any joy or sense of purpose.

"Do you mean that or are you just saying it to shut me up? If you don't really love me, don't say that you do."

"What do you want from me, Alison?"

"I want the truth, Dusty."

"Fine. Truth is you're the only person I care about and I would be lost without you. It feels right when you're with me. Like it was meant to be."

"And…?"

"*And…?* I don't know what else you want me to say."

"If I have to tell you what to say then it isn't worth it. I want you to love me like I love you, Dusty. Unconditionally. When you can do that, give me a call."

And with that she rose from the couch, grabbed her belongings and left without so much as a goodbye.

I moped around for weeks. Alison was the only person I knew in Texas, outside of my family, and I was miserable without her. Making friends wasn't something I was good at, partly because I was introverted and shy, but more so because my mother had made a lot of those choices on my behalf. Trust issues were most assuredly another contributing factor as to why I was friendless.

I replayed our last moments together over and over and couldn't understand why she was so angry with me. It made absolutely no sense, whatsoever. She asked me to be honest and I was. I *did* love her, as unconditionally as I knew how. I may not have uttered the actual words but my actions should have proven otherwise.

Another month passed and I could tell she wasn't going to apologize so I did, even though, deep down, I knew I didn't mean it. Was that how our relationship was going to be? Me saying what she wanted to hear in order for her to be happy? Short answer to that was "yes." And so began my mastery of knowing *what* to say to satisfy a woman, coupled with the bigger reward of knowing *when* to say it.

We were barely reunited a month when her parents began raising concerns over the amount of time we were spending together. I'm sure they knew just how close we had actually become. In an attempt to put distance between us, they ordered her to focus her attention more on boys and less on me. They also told her they weren't going to pay for her college unless she started dating. Or at least that's what she told me.

With each boyfriend we grew further apart, a realism that didn't seem to bother her as it did me. I truly believed having her in my life in some limited capacity was better than not having her at all, so I accepted the role of second string with little resistance. Every once in a while, I would buck the system and break up with her and she would always beg me to come back. And I did. Every time.

We stayed together, more off than on, for another eighteen months when I finally threw in the towel for good, convinced that "crazy little thing called love" wasn't all it was cracked up to be. I wanted a more transient way of life, with no ties to anyone. Uncle Sam offered me a new set of walking shoes. I tried them on and found they were a perfect fit.

— THESE BOOTS ARE MADE FOR WALKING —

A flurry of brief, insignificant daydreams transpired in the weeks following the first two, and although they weren't as unnerving as the previous pair, they were still intent on perpetuating the ills of my childhood. A few days later, another one occurred. There was no movie screen or teenager in this dream, only a calendar on the table with the date set to October 4, 1979, and the Army Caisson song blaring out from the darkness.

At nineteen I joined the Army, not quite a kid anymore but still years away from real maturity. Young and naïve, I was clueless to the homophobes in uniform around me. It all became perfectly clear when I tried to out another girl during Basic Training and was immediately reprimanded for assuming she was, as she so delicately put it, "a fucking queer."

It wasn't okay to be gay in the military, everyone knew that, but I thought I could at least forge a friendship with someone who was so obviously like me. Couldn't make that kind of mistake again or I might wind up with an invitation to a trial by court-martial. I thought being a lesbian was the neatest thing since sliced bread. I guess everyone else didn't see it the same way.

Throughout my first year I managed to sneak lovers in and out of the barracks with great finesse. Once inside, however, silence was mandatory because noises permeated the paper-thin walls like water through a sieve. Some of my dorm mates were already acting suspicious of my orientation. It would have been curtains for me if any of them heard the sounds of same sex partners coming from my room. Unfortunately, there was no escape from the insufferable racket of their sexual encounters with men. "Fuck me!" they would wail. "Harder! That's it! Put it in me! Deeper, baby! Deeper! Don't stop! Right there! Faster! Faster! Oh God! *I'M C-O-M-I-N-N-G-G-G!*"

Their moaning and groaning had no consequence, which I found to be prejudicially unfair, so one night I took revenge by smuggling a rather feisty woman into my bed. My instincts told me she would be trouble, but she was *HOT* and that seemed to have more importance in the bigger scheme of things.

Within minutes the little redhead became a screamer, the type of lover that always made me fearful of getting caught. Although I enjoyed living on the edge with my lesbian trysts, my future in the military would be jeopardized if I couldn't quiet this one down.

While my date continued to vocalize louder than any before her, I had an epiphany.

If we were in a '69' position, her mouth would be occupied and the noises coming from her would be muted. Hmmm...

With lightning speed, I flipped around and climbed on top of her. She was confused at first, but quickly reverted back into action once her face was nestled between my legs. The only sounds emitted thereafter were muffled, making my plan a complete success.

From that day forward, '69' took its ranking as the most pleasurable way to silence any sexual threats to my military career.

- -

My tour of duty lasted a total of eight and a half years, during which time I met many lesbians, thanks to Uncle Sam. I also *did* many lesbians, thanks again to Uncle Sam. Annual sporting events were like lesbian smorgasbords with women flown in from every corner of the world. It was no secret a great majority of them were gay.

The expression "too many women, too little time" was rumored to have originated at one of our tournaments. While it wasn't possible to sleep with every eligible lesbian, I had more than a reasonable share over the years.

A lot of women knew me, not just for my talent on the field but for my reputation in the bedroom as well. I was proud to be a "Player" both in sports and in life and wore that title like a soldier wears the coveted Congressional Medal of Honor.

My reputation (and arrogance) allowed me to believe that I could have any woman from any sporting event. My prowess, however, was challenged at the 1986 championship softball tournament as I spent the first three days of the weeklong playoffs trying to get between the sheets with a petite, hot-bodied shortstop from Fort Benning, a woman who apparently wanted nothing to do with me. My friends, not used to seeing me night after night at these events, began to insinuate I had lost my touch. I knew my abilities were still intact and set out to prove it.

The shortstop, Ann Marie, was a softball legend, having held the record for the most consecutive nominations to the Army's elite women's All-Star team. Everyone was anxious to see her play and I was no exception.

The attractive shortstop waved me off every time I tried to talk to her. Having never been turned down before, each dismissal fueled my determination to jump right back in and give it another try. I was convinced my irresistible charm would prevail, as it always had in the past, but my window of opportunity was diminishing with each passing day. In less than forty-eight hours the tournament would be over and we would all be sent home.

Ann Marie's team lost in the semifinal round. My team played in the matchup that followed and she and her teammates were still in the dugout when I strolled in and laid my bag on the bench. I lifted a bottle of water from the side pocket and offered it to her. Sparks flew from her eyes as she snubbed her nose and turned away. Her refusal was over the top, dramatically staged for everyone within sight.

I can play the drama card, too, I mused, reaching past her and handing the bottle to one of her teammates, playing up the pretense that this little spitfire wasn't the object of my attention after all. My friends on the team, all still waiting to come inside, offered a thumbs-up to signal their endorsement.

Good thing I never told them who I was really after, I mugged.

Mary, Ann Marie's teammate, smiled and accepted my gift willingly. While she wasn't the type I usually went for, in that particular moment I didn't care. I merely needed her to save face.

Within the span of a few minutes she became a chatterbox, rattling off about things that were of absolutely no interest to me. The more she talked, the more I disliked her. I was mere seconds from leaving the dugout when she asked if I wanted to join her later for a "last night in town" party in Ann Marie's room.

What? Another chance at Ann Marie?

I smiled and accepted without hesitation.

Our game ended with a win and I hurried to clean up after, hoping for time alone with Ann Marie before the festivities began. Grabbing a six-pack from the fridge, I rushed over to her building. As luck would have it, I was the first to arrive.

She greeted me at the door in a pair of baggy shorts and a loose-fitting top. I could tell she wasn't wearing a bra, and my overactive imagination assured me she was probably naked underneath her shorts as well.

"Mary told me you were coming," she said, leaning against the jamb. My eyes were fixed on her breasts as she spoke. "She's not here yet but I can get her for you. Her room is just down the hall."

She cleared her throat to divert my attention away from her chest. I looked into her eyes, now soft and welcoming, quite the opposite of the daggers that bore holes through mine earlier in the dugout.

The light from the hallway cast a small halo around her face, which only served to accentuate her magnificent features. Looking at her rendered me speechless. When the words finally did come, I was as tongue-tied as I had been in my first conversation with Celeste those many years ago.

"I, uh, I mean, you don't, uh…" Then I sighed, causing her to laugh.

She motioned for me to enter and I handed her a beer in passing. Assuming Mary was the reason I couldn't speak, Ann Marie chuckled and said, "I have a tough time finding the right words to say when Mary's name comes up in conversation, too. Glad to know she has the same effect on someone else. She's cute but not overly bright. Know what I mean?"

After gathering my wits, I confessed, "I didn't come to see Mary."

"Really? So why are you here?"

"Something to do, I guess."

"Yeah, you're right. There really isn't much to do around here except play ball."

"That's not true. There are lots of things to do besides that."

"Such as?"

"Let's talk when the party's over. Right now, there's something I want to ask you."

"Okay."

"I've tried all week to talk to you but you've given me the cold shoulder. Why?"

"You seemed desperate. I don't like that."

"Sorry. I was on a deadline."

"Excuse me? What does that mean?"

"Nothing. Forget it."

She crossed her arms and frowned before speaking again.

"I watched your game this afternoon and your team is good. Good enough to win the tournament. You're an excellent pitcher, Dusty, and there's talk among the coaches about nominating you for the All-Star team."

"Wow! That's fantastic! Thanks for telling me!"

"Your name was also mentioned by several players, but I sensed it wasn't because of your ability to throw a knuckle ball."

"It's probably the other things I do on the mound that impresses them."

"Come again? What you 'do on the mound?'"

My response was preempted by a knock on the door. Ann Marie opened it and was nearly trampled by her teammates as they charged into the room. Mary shoved her way through the pack and came rushing toward me.

"You're here!" she shrieked, throwing her arms around my neck. "I'm so glad you came!"

"So am I," I replied.

Glancing over Mary's shoulder, I smiled at Ann Marie. Not long after, I caught her smiling back at me.

The first thirty minutes with Mary were tolerable, but in all the time that followed I was bored out of my mind. I felt suffocated and needed some air. Ann Marie would have to wait; I had to get out of there. Pushing Mary aside, I made my way to the door. As if on cue, Ann Marie rose to her feet at the same time and raised her hands to quiet the crowd.

"It's been a long day," she announced. "I hate to break this up but I think I'm ready for bed. Thanks for coming, ladies. I'll see you all tomorrow."

Mary hurried to my side, eager to snag me before I got away.

"We can continue the party in my room since she's throwing us out," she said. "I've got beer."

"I can't," I answered gruffly, frustrated that I had to speak to her at all. "I have an early game and need to get some rest."

"What about after the game? We're out of the competition so they're flying us out tomorrow evening. Maybe we could squeeze some time in before…"

"I don't know, Mary. If my team loses, we might have to play back-to-back games. Better ask me again tomorrow, okay?"

She hugged me before teetering off in the direction of her room. As the rest of her teammates staggered past me, I shouted a sincere "thanks" to Ann Marie.

"You're welcome," she replied, her voice raised to carry over the din.

I had barely made it to the exit door when I heard her call out, "Dusty! Wait up!"

I quickly turned around and made my way back to where she was standing.

"What time is your game tomorrow?" she asked.

"Eight o'clock. Why?"

"Just curious." She eyed me for a moment then added, "What time is it now?"

I glanced at my watch. "It's a little after eleven."

"Are you tired? You want to stay and watch TV?"

"You've got a TV in your room? My room doesn't have…"

"Calm down, stud. Did you *see* a TV in my room?"

"Um, no. Can't say that I did. So, if we're not going to watch TV then what..."

"Don't play dumb, Dusty. You mentioned other things to do besides playing ball."

I strutted past her, grinning as I made my way into her room, suddenly realizing the energy I had spent on her might not have been wasted after all.

She followed me inside and closed the door behind us. Her lips quickly made their way onto mine as we shuffled in awkward, tangled steps toward the bed. I leaned into her, hoping to ease her onto her back but she grabbed the front of my shirt and tossed me onto the covers instead.

"Not so fast," I grinned. "I'm not that easy."

"Please. That's not what I've been told."

"Does that mean you've been asking about me?"

She ignored my question and latched onto the side of my neck and I immediately felt the life forces being drained from my body as a powerful vacuum occurred in the space between my skin and her tongue. I tried to pull away but she had me pinned against the bed.

This is my *conquest,* I thought. *I need to be the one in control here.*

I can't explain how it happened, but I somehow managed to position myself on top of her. Her muscular legs immediately locked around my waist, tightening and releasing, her pelvic bones grinding against mine with each thrust of her hips. I slid my hand inside of her shorts and, just as I had imagined when she met me at the door, she wasn't wearing anything underneath.

This was definitely going to be the biggest score of my life. She was, after all, Ann Marie, the crème de la crème of lesbians. Those who had wagered in my favor would not be disappointed tonight. Hands down, I was going to win back my reputation.

I moved to the floor, kneeling while kissing the soft flesh of her inner thighs. Beads of perspiration formed across my lip as my nose burrowed its way through her pubic hair. Her hips began to move faster, rhythmically gliding back and forth. I tongued her clit and pushed two fingers inside of her. The climax that followed was fast and furious.

After her orgasm, I snuggled in behind her and draped my arm over her waist. My mind was racing, imagining all sorts of pleasures she would offer me in return. Instead of indulging any of those fantasies she glanced over her shoulder and muttered, "You should go now."

I kissed the base of her neck, pretending not to hear.

"Dusty," she said a little louder. "You need to leave."

"Why? Is something wrong?"

"You ask too many questions. Just go."

Lifting up on one elbow, I glared at her.

"What is with you?"

"Good night," she growled.

"Whatever," I snarled in return.

The entire trip back to my barracks was spent trying to figure out what could have caused Ann Marie's mood to change as drastically as it had. Confused and frustrated, I hurled my tired body onto the bed. Her words haunted me throughout the remainder of the night and well into the next morning.

After hours of tossing and turning I finally got up and dressed for the game, still dazed by all that had transpired. Linda, my roommate, who was also a lesbian, eyed me with a puzzled expression as I came out of the bathroom.

"Wow, Dusty. What happened to you?"

"What do you mean?"

She touched the bloodstained mark on the side of my neck and giggled.

"I think the vampire needed a better map to your carotid artery."

Slapping her hand, I roughly brushed past her.

"Hold up," she said. "I'll grab a quick shower and walk with you to the field."

"Okay. Not to rub it in, but I'm really tired from the action I got last night. Mind if we play a little catch when we get there so I can loosen up a bit?"

"You are such a whore dog, Dusty."

"Whatever. Hurry up and get ready. I'll wait for you outside."

Linda continued to poke fun as we traveled the short distance to the ballpark. Mary was already on the field when we arrived, waiting at the entrance to the dugout. As we got closer, I swear that hickey must have jumped right off my body and smacked her squarely across the face.

"Thought you were tired," she hissed, pointing at my neck. "Isn't that what you said last night? So, whose bed did you end up in? Was it Ann Marie's?"

"That's none of your business, Mary."

"Fuck you. You are such a bitch, Dusty."

She stormed away while I scanned the bleachers, hopeful there was no one around to witness her meltdown. Ann Marie was the only person in the stands, of course, sitting alone behind the opponent's dugout.

"Wait a minute," Linda said. "I'm confused. That's the chick you gave the water to yesterday, but she isn't the one you got it on with last night?"

"No, it wasn't Mary."

"Who was it then?"

I nodded in the direction of Ann Marie.

"You are shitting me! You had sex with *her?* The shortstop?"

I giggled as though I had been caught making out with my high school P.E. teacher in the locker room after practice.

"Yeah, I slept with Ann Marie."

"You dog. How is it you always get the hottest chicks at these things?"

"Just lucky, I guess."

"Lucky my ass. There has to be something in that cologne of yours. Some kind of pheromone, maybe. Mind if I borrow some tonight?"

"Sure. But don't be mad if it doesn't work for you."

"Okay. And don't *you* be mad if it does."

She patted me on the shoulder and laughed. Reaching into her bag, she pulled out a ball and tossed it in my direction.

"Let's get that hot butt of yours on the mound and warm up."

"I need to run over and talk to Ann Marie first, okay?"

"Sure. Some of the others are coming, so I'll just hang out here."

"Thanks, Linda."

I sprinted across the infield and scaled the bleachers two at a time, taking a seat on the row in front of Ann Marie.

"Hello," I said cautiously, still reeling from her earlier dismissal. "How are you?"

"I'm fine," she answered with a bite.

"What is it with you? Why are you acting like this?"

"Like what?"

"Like you did before last night. What happened?"

"Don't flatter yourself, honey. I didn't come here to find a lover. I came to play ball. Drinking makes me horny and I had a lot to drink last night. That's all."

I glared at her but didn't respond, knowing there were no words to adequately retaliate with. Although I wasn't as direct or harsh as she was, on the inside we were two of a kind. She played me, just as I had played the many conquests in my past.

Guilt stabbed at my heart as I began to consider how many women hated me for the same reasons I now hated Ann Marie.

- -

After the tournament I took a long, hard look at my life and realized it was time for a change. It sickened me to think of how many women I had taken advantage of in order to be considered one of the elites.

Convinced I could achieve the same harmony as my coupled friends, I decided to leave the single life behind and embark on a more meaningful relationship. Considering the hordes of women available at the tournaments, I didn't think finding a mate would prove to be that difficult. I shared my intentions with my friends and then set my sights toward the most logical hangouts. The neighborhood bars.

Either I strolled in overly obvious or one of my friends sent out an early warning because every woman in the bar seemed to know I was on the prowl. All of the unclaimed lesbians within a fifty-mile radius must have run for the hills or simply vanished from the face of the earth. This was going to be harder than I thought. How much easier it had been to find a partner when I wasn't playing for keeps.

I cruised the bars for nearly six months before scoring any real success, having all but given up on finding a permanent love. On a cold, wet, January night I ran into a former third baseman from my softball team. Tiffany was a sweet piece of eye candy with athletic legs and the best-looking arms in softball. Tall, dark haired and dark eyed, she could have easily landed a starring role in any lesbian fantasy.

She and her partner, Julie, had been together for five years. Assuming Julie was somewhere nearby, I asked about her. Tiffany's face quickly soured and she began to cry. It would have been rude to leave her alone in that state so I stayed and listened while she poured out her heart and soul.

As the story was told, Julie booked a motel without Tiffany's knowledge and, in her haste, forgot to take the receipt out of her pants pocket. Tiffany found it that night while doing laundry, so she decided to drive to the motel and check it out. Julie answered the door wrapped in a towel while her lover stayed in the bed, all clearly visible from where she was standing.

Tiffany decided the only way to erase the image was to drink it away and she had made definite progress on that front by the time I arrived. Her depressed state made me feel obliged to hang around until things got better. It was an obligation that would last for seven long years.

Nine days after meeting at the bar, I let Tiffany move in with me. It all made perfect sense at the time. She didn't want to stay in the same apartment with her cheating partner and I had an extra room, so…

She fell hard for me and was sleeping in my bed by the end of the third week. I tried to muster feelings for her as well but it was no use. It was then I realized I had made the biggest mistake of my life. I didn't love Tiffany. Maybe some infatuation, but it definitely wasn't love.

The outcome of behavior modification appeared bleak at best but I had committed myself and would never go back on my word. I decided to try harder to make things work, hoping that over time I would grow to love her. And eventually, I did. Like a really good friend. With benefits.

In December of the following year, the Army's Office of Special Investigations set a trap to catch suspected homosexuals. Tiffany had already separated from the service, so she was safe. I wasn't. Rumors spread quickly through the gay grapevine that my name was on the list. Sure enough, I received an official order from the Commander to appear for questioning not long after the investigation began.

One of the attorneys at the interrogation looked familiar though I couldn't recall specifically when or where we had met. At certain times during the proceedings she would interrupt by reminding everyone present that I had not been formally charged with any wrongdoing. After an hour of questioning, she asked for a short recess. I followed her into the restroom where she offered an opinion of what would likely happen upon our return.

"Listen," she said, her voice barely louder than a whisper. "I could get in big trouble for doing this, but you need to know we have enough substantiating evidence in there to end your military career. If this goes to a court-martial, and I'm assuming it will, you are looking at a Dishonorable Discharge. There are sworn affidavits from a host of women attesting to your homosexuality. When we go back, don't say anything to incriminate yourself. Instead, say, 'I choose not to respond without an attorney present for my defense.' Once you ask for an attorney, the investigators are legally obligated to stop the interrogation. Understand?"

I grimaced and lowered my eyes, nodding slowly.

"Good. They are likely to get suspicious if we don't return soon. I only have time to say this once so pay close attention. Okay?"

I looked directly into her eyes and nodded again.

"I'm going to offer you a chance to explain. When I do, admit that you have been seen in the company of the women who were discharged. Say nothing more on the subject. I will then produce the affidavits for you to read. Don't say anything after reading them. Once you have finished, I will present you with an option for early release from your military commitment, to which you will agree."

"But…"

"Don't interrupt. I can get you a General Discharge under Honorable Conditions if you accept the terms I am offering. If not, you could be forced out, or worse, face jail time, reduction in rank or pay forfeiture if they decide to prosecute. I see this as your only way out."

"I guess I don't really have a choice. My career is over whether I like it or not."

"Do you have any questions before we go back?"

"Only one. Have we met before? You look very familiar to me."

"I meant questions about the investigation. Do you want to ask anything relevant to these proceedings?"

"No. You've sufficiently explained everything."

"Let's get back in there. Remember, don't say anything to incriminate yourself."

"Wait. I do have another question."

"What is it?"

"Will you be my lawyer?"

"I have already been assigned to the prosecution. I can call a defense attorney from the Base Legal Office if that is what you want, but I don't think it will matter much if this goes to trial. I'm sorry, Dusty. There is just too much evidence against you."

My eyes were glued to the floor the entire walk back to the interrogation room. As she reached for the door, she very quickly turned and whispered over her shoulder, "We met a year and a half ago at the softball tournament at Fort Benning."

"I remember now! Mary…"

"Shush, Dusty. Not another word."

"I understand. Thanks for the advice. I really appreciate it."

Everything progressed as Mary predicted and I was processed out of the military with a General Discharge. Though I dreaded the thought of trading in my battle dress uniform and combat boots for a business suit and pumps, it was better than the alternative of a striped jumpsuit with ball and chain accessories.

- - - - - - - - - - - - - - - - - - -

My military experiences helped me land a job in the Government sector as a federal contractor. Time moved steadily along for Tiffany and I without any major disruptions for the next few years. Sometime around our fourth anniversary she launched a business of her own as a personal trainer. I lost my job due to budget cuts the year that followed and her inexperience as an entrepreneur led to the demise of her venture not long afterwards. We watched helplessly as our home went from a castle to a cave, nearly all of our personal possessions sold in order to stay afloat.

Tiffany wanted a fresh start somewhere far removed from Maryland. For reasons unbeknownst to me she chose Texas. So here I was back in the land of Alison and the she-devil, a place I swore I would never set foot in again.

Tiffany was an administrative assistant in the military and found a position right away as an office manager at a print shop. I wasn't as fortunate. The Lone Star state didn't have much need for a tactical communications specialist, and a female one at that. After numerous interviews and countless hand-delivered resumes I wasn't any closer to being hired than I was when I applied for my first job at the Post Office when I was thirteen.

Six months later, with still no real progress on the job front, I was worried that my unemployment benefits would expire before finding work. Mere hours before collecting my final check, Tiffany phoned to say that the graphic artist where she worked had quit without notice and that Bob (the owner) and Kathy (the sales manager) were in a pinch to find a replacement fast. She had convinced them I would be a good candidate because of my computer skills, and, after meeting, Bob said he would give me a chance. What he actually gave me was a new lease on life.

—— A Toast To Love ——

It had been nearly a year since the last daydream and I was convinced my life was finally back on track. Bob was still my boss, but Tiffany and I were no longer a couple. She and I stayed employed together until the summer of 1994, when, four months shy of our seventh anniversary, she ended our relationship and quit her job – all on the same day. Bob and I were equally blindsided; neither of us knew of her plans beforehand. She simply walked out of our lives as though she had never been in them.

I dated a few women after that but didn't stay involved for very long. They wanted permanency. I didn't. In the early days with Tiffany, I promised myself that if I was ever single again, I wouldn't commit to another relationship until I was ready. Also, my next partner had to be someone *I* loved, not just someone who loved me. That hadn't happened yet, and it didn't look like it was going to occur anytime in the foreseeable future.

- - - - - - - - - - - - - - - - - - - -

With Tiffany gone I was the only homosexual on staff, and, quite possibly, the only gay person in my coworkers' lives, so they affectionately dubbed me the "Token Queer," which I found oddly endearing. Maggie and Beth serviced the lobby and front counter, answering incoming calls and greeting walk-in customers. When she wasn't out meeting prospective clients, Kathy would come to the front when there was more traffic than the two of them could handle; otherwise, she stayed in her office making sales calls. She had been on staff the longest, working for Bob since the store's opening ten years earlier. Beth was hired the fifth year, and Tiffany and I came on board two years after that. Six months after we started, Maggie joined the team.

My office was located behind a big pane of glass that separated the lobby from the production area. As the store's graphic artist, I was responsible for designing letterheads, business cards, and promotional signs and banners, and I occasionally helped out Maggie and Beth with boxing up the finished products.

Working with those two was a blast. Kathy, on the other hand, had to be taken with a grain of salt. She was a moody gal who could be quite unpredictable at times. Beth told me that she was a former alcoholic and drug user, but was also a lifelong friend of Bob's and he had the utmost confidence in her abilities. She didn't disappoint, generating seven-figure revenues year after year. She wasn't going anywhere.

Beth was the office cut up. Without a doubt, she was the funniest person I had ever known. Her dry wit and humor were uniquely her own, and she could make people laugh over just about any topic. Maggie wasn't the brightest star in the galaxy, but she was a lot of fun to be around as well. She and Beth were a hoot, always ragging each other over one thing or another. Beth also had a serious side that only came out on rare occasions, such as the day she shared her innermost thoughts with me.

"You know," she started, "when I was a little girl, I dreamed that I would grow up and marry a really handsome guy, have 2.5 kids…"

"2.5 kids?" I interrupted. "How is that possible?"

"Stay with the story, Dusty."

"Sorry. Please continue."

"My husband was the bank president in town and we lived in a huge mansion with a wrought iron gate at the entrance to our property."

"Whoa, girl! When you dream, you sure dream big!"

"Damn straight! Oops… Is that an offensive thing to say to a lesbian?"

"It's fine, Beth. Go on with your story."

"I have always had big goals for myself. Don't get me wrong, I love Dan and couldn't imagine my life without him, but he is not a banker and we will never live in a mansion. I'm not sure if we'll ever have kids, either."

"How long have you two been together?"

"Five years."

"Doesn't he want the same things as you?"

"I thought he did in the beginning. Now I'm not so sure."

"You should tell him how you feel, Beth."

"I know. I'm just afraid it will scare him off."

"I've seen the way he looks at you whenever he comes around. I don't think there's anything you could say that would make him leave you."

"I don't care about being rich, though it would be nice, but I have always wanted to get married and have children."

"Has Dan ever proposed?"

"No."

"Why don't you propose to him?"

"Be serious, Dusty. Women don't propose to men."

"Why not? My cousin did and she's been happily married for years now!"

"I'll give it some thought."

"I think you should do it, Beth. I'm sure he'll say yes. He'd be a fool not to!"

"Thanks, Dusty. What about you? Did you have dreams when you were young?"

"Yeah. I dreamed that I probably wouldn't survive to see my next birthday."

"Why? Did you have a bad childhood?"

"You could say that."

"Well, I think you've recovered magnificently!"

"In some respects. I still have trust issues."

"What Tiffany did to you would justify having trust issues."

"She was just the icing on the cake."

"Do you dream now?"

"Strangely enough, I started having these weird daydreams not long after she left."

"About Tiffany?"

"No. About my life; from the time I was four until I was discharged from the Army."

"Were they happy daydreams?"

"Partly. But the bad stuff was in there, too."

"Are you still having them?"

"No, thank goodness. They stopped about six months ago."

"I remember you after Tiffany left. You were so broken. I'm glad you were able to put that behind you and move on."

"Thanks, Beth. It hasn't been easy. I know I still have a long way to go."

"Now that we've shared our deepest, darkest secrets, I say we go next door and get a drink to lift our spirits. My treat!"

"From the burger joint?" I laughingly quipped.

"Sure! But first I need to tell the warden. You know how Kathy gets when she can't find us."

She picked up the phone and dialed Kathy's extension.

"Dusty and I are stepping out for a minute," she announced. "Maggie can cover the front until we get back."

A momentary pause ensued, then, "All right. We won't be gone long."

I followed her out of the store and into the restaurant. After getting our drinks, she raised her glass high above her head.

"I would like to make a toast," she said.

I raised my glass in return and tapped my straw against hers.

"May all of our dreams lead us to our one true love," she said.

"A toast to love," I replied enthusiastically. "I'll drink to that!"

When we returned to the store, she linked her arm through mine and escorted me to my office.

"I'm going to make it my mission to find you a mate," she announced as I lowered myself into my chair. "Pretty women come in here all the time and I'm sure one of them could be a match for you. If not in real life, then at least in your dreams. You could indulge in a different fantasy every night of the week!"

A slight giggle escaped me as I shook my head from side to side. Moments later, a "ding" sounded to alert us that someone had entered the store. When I looked up, I saw a blonde-haired beauty walking up to the counter. Beth saw her, too, then turned to me and said in a boisterous voice, "And we're off!"

I watched to see if she would own up to the challenge and the smile I got from the customer let me know that she had. After that, every time an attractive woman came into the store she would tap on the glass to get my attention. And, every night that followed I would see that same woman in my dreams.

— — — — — — — — — — — — — — — — — —

I had purposely stopped having meals at the diner because it seemed to be a trigger for my daydreams. I still got my food there on occasion, but only to go. Mabel was always inviting me to stay but I didn't want to tempt fate and kick things off again, so I made up flimsy excuses as to why I couldn't.

"I miss talking with you," she told me one night.

"Awww... I miss you, too! You're right. It's time that I get back among the living."

"I'm not sure that's how I would characterize what's in here tonight. They're more like a pack of zombies."

She pointed out a group of teenagers layered in dark clothes with black eyeshadow, black lipstick and black fingernails. Two of the teens had metal rods protruding from the edge of their eyebrows.

"That's the fad nowadays," I responded. "It's called 'goth'."

"Yeah, well... No matter what they call themselves, it still looks freaky to me."

She offered more of her thoughts in a hushed voice as she ushered me to my booth.

"Take that boy over there with the skull and crossbones tattoo on his neck. Doesn't he remind you of the Grim Reaper?"

Grinning, I replied, "That's not a boy, Mabel."

"Are you kidding me?" she snapped. Her eyes were fixed on the teen as she spoke. "What the hell is wrong with girls today?"

She exhaled loudly, shaking her head as she lifted her order pad from the pocket of her apron and plucked a pencil from behind her ear.

"Guess I'm showing my age again. You'd never catch anyone from my generation doing crap like that."

"You know, that might be just what they need to snap them out of it. Seeing one of their parents dressed like that would probably scare the goth right out of them!"

We shared a laugh before Mabel asked, "What'll it be tonight, honey? It's Thursday, so you know what that means."

"Meatloaf..." I groaned.

Mabel nodded.

"No thanks. I'll stick with my usual."

"You got it! Grilled cheese with extra dill pickles. Want some fries with that? Benny just pulled a fresh batch out of the fryer."

"That's okay. Just the sandwich is fine."

I paused for a moment then rubbed my chin and modified my response.

"No wait. I'll have some onion rings, too."

"Okie doke. I'll get this right out to you. You want tea or Pepsi to drink with that?"

"I'll have tea. Thanks, Mabel."

Within seconds of her departure, I felt the walls start to close in around me.

"Oh no you don't!" I growled. "Just back away and leave me alone!"

When Mabel returned with my drink, she sensed that something had changed.

"Are you all right?" she asked. "You look like you're about to pass out."

"There's something about this diner that always seems to put me in a trance."

"Wouldn't doubt it," she responded with a smile and a quick wink. "This place gives me hallucinations. Listen, doll. I've got to go tend to the goths. I'll be back with your food in a jiff."

I waited for her leave then reached in my pocket and pulled out a half-empty pack of cigarettes. I lit one and inhaled slowly, allowing the vapors to trail out without exerting very much of my own air. With each puff that followed, I felt my eyelids growing heavier.

I smoked the cigarette down to the filter and mashed it in the ashtray then watched as the last of the ashes burned completely out. I was struggling to stay conscious when my food arrived and barely managed to get a "thank you" out to Mabel before the dream took hold and transported me back into the darkness.

- -

This daydream was unlike any other in that it lasted only a few seconds. There were no characters, screen or music, just the calendar, which was set to November 18, 1996.

How bizarre, I thought. *That date is more than a year away…*

I finished my meal and stopped for an ice cream on my way home. I still felt stuffed when I went to bed an hour later, which typically resulted in my having bad dreams. But there were several gorgeous women that visited the store that day and my hope was that they would be the only things on my mind that night.

As I drifted off to sleep, the word "bizarre" kept repeating itself in my brain.

—— LIFE IS BUT A DREAM ——

It was a slow workday, unusual for the week leading up to Thanksgiving. Kathy was making sales calls, but Beth and Maggie and I were basically left with nothing to do. There hadn't been one customer all morning, so we passed the time tidying things up around the production area. When that was done, we started gossiping. I was about to launch into a new lesbian tale when a particularly striking woman entered the store. Beth saw that my mouth was hanging open as she came toward us, so she jabbed me in the ribs with her elbow and whispered, "Dusty. Shut your trap."

Maggie smiled at the fair-skinned beauty and asked, "Can I help you?"

The lovely creature smiled in return, prompting large dimples to appear on either side of her face. Her golden, silky hair swayed back and forth across the top of her breasts as she approached the counter.

My heart began to beat erratically and my feet felt like they were giving up on their assignment, which, quite simply, was to keep me standing. Thank God I still had strength in my arms and managed to hold myself up despite the mutiny occurring below my knees.

"Hello," the woman said. "I'm here to pick up my order. I believe all of those boxes in the corner are mine. Could one of you help me carry them to my car?"

"I will!" I declared, eagerly volunteering before Beth or Maggie had the chance.

I stepped from behind the counter and gathered all eight boxes at once, hoping to impress the beautiful stranger with my brute strength. The adrenaline coursing through my body could have empowered me to lift the brick building I worked in, if she had asked.

I followed her to a vintage Ford Mustang (1965 by the looks of it) parked alongside Bob's brand-new Lexus. She opened the passenger door then turned to collect the top box from the stack I was holding. Her skirt slid up as she bent down to set it on the floorboard, offering me a revealing peak at her backside. I was craning my neck for a better view when Kathy came out and told me to behave or go back inside. I had little doubt that she had been summoned by Maggie and Beth as I glanced back at the store and caught the two of them laughing and pointing at me from the lobby.

The only plausible excuse I could think to tell Kathy was that the distorted angle of my head was due to a recurring injury that had plagued me since childhood. She knew it was a load of crap and opted to stay put until the customer departed, just in case it became necessary to protect the store's dignity and integrity from any inappropriate behavior on my part.

"Thank you," the woman said after placing the final box. Her voice was deep and sultry and hearing it made my knees weak all over again. I'm sure I looked like a drooling idiot standing there in that parking lot.

"Would it be possible for you to come to my store and help me unload these?" she asked. Tossing her hair over her shoulder, she added, "It's not far from here."

Even though my "gaydar" didn't register a hit, I couldn't help but feel that she was flirting with me.

Why not? I pondered, then reasoned, *What the hell?*

I barely got the word "Sure" out before Kathy interjected, "Sorry, that isn't allowed. Our insurance only covers us on these premises."

The woman smiled and a flawless row of pearly white teeth emerged.

"I understand," she said, still grinning.

Kathy thanked her for her order and headed back to the store alone. As I turned to follow, the woman reached out and touched my shoulder. Then she moved a step closer and lowered her hand to my forearm. We were now within inches of one another.

"Maybe you could come by after work," she said, still holding my arm. "I could pay you in cash so your boss would never have to know."

"Thanks, but I couldn't take your money."

"What about something besides money? Would that change your mind?"

What a tempting proposition, I mused. *But helping her could cost me my job and I can't risk being unemployed again.*

From out of nowhere, a tiny Queen Fairy appeared on my shoulder dressed in a red vest with matching tights and a pink feather boa draped loosely around his neck, twirling a small pitchfork as though it were a baton. His thick, black curls reminded me of Alison's favorite singer, Gino Vanelli, bouncing up and down as he tossed the pitchfork back and forth between his hands.

"Don't stand there like an ass!" he hissed. He then glared at me before adding, "Let me point out that you haven't had any horizontal action in a long time. An *extremely* long time. This kind of hotness doesn't fall out of the sky every day, you know."

Before I could respond or even comprehend his presence, his nemesis, an Angel, made herself known on my other shoulder. She appeared to be quite the little lesbian with a chain of keys dangling from her belt loop and a pair of black, scuffed biker boots sticking out from the bottom of her tattered jeans. Her muscle-bound arms were crossed over one another atop an oversized belt buckle, her eyebrows arched in such a way that I knew my chances of having anything to do with this attractive stranger were relatively nil.

I considered the Queen Fairy's argument for a moment then begrudgingly thanked the woman and again said no. He responded by poking me in the neck with his pitchfork.

"No?" he piped. "Are you nuts? The correct answer is yes, Dusty. Repeat after me. 'Y-E-S.' Say yes, you big dope! You're blowing your chance here, missy!"

"That's okay," the woman said, seemingly disappointed as her smile turned into a pouty frown. "I'll just get my brother to help me."

"I'm sorry. We appreciate your business and I hope that you'll come back again."

"Oh, I'm quite sure I'll be back."

She offered a quick flip of her wrist from the driver's seat as she sped away. After she was gone, I rebuked the Queen Fairy with a snarly remark of my own.

"See? All is well that ends well. You heard her. She said she'd be back."

"Yeah," he grumbled, rolling his eyes with an exaggerated flair. "I heard her. That's what they all say. I swear, girlfriend. Haven't you learned anything from your past?"

Mimicking the Scarecrow in The Wizard of Oz, he began to croon, "This would be a whole lot simpler and you just might get a tickler if you only had a brain."

"Watch it," I challenged. "I'm not sure where you came from but I'm betting that I can send you back there."

"Play nice, Dusty. You may think you don't need me now, but there will soon come a time when you'll be begging for my help."

"Yeah. Like that will ever happen."

Walking back to the office I could see my coworkers huddled together, gearing up to pounce as soon as I came inside. I hesitated pulling the handle, fearing the barrage of questions that would begin before the door had time to close behind me.

And I was right.

Beth: "She was some kinda hot, Dusty. Did you get her number?"

Kathy: "Please tell me you didn't ask her for a date. Did you?"

Maggie: "She didn't look gay to me. How did you know she was a lesbian?"

"We have a secret code word," I answered mockingly. "Homosexuals are the only ones that know what it is."

"Really?" Maggie challenged. She seemed genuinely shocked that I hadn't shared that level of detail with her before. "Better tell me what it is, Dusty, in case someone says it to me one day."

Kathy patted her on the back and said, "I'm not seeing that card in your Tarot deck, Maggie."

Knowing that Maggie was being serious, I bit my lip to stifle my own laughter.

"You are such a doof," Beth chided. "She's pulling your leg, Maggie." Her eyes then shifted from Maggie to me. "You are pulling her leg, aren't you, Dusty?"

I smiled and quickly walked past, refusing any further conversation. All the while, the Queen Fairy was continuing his rampage about wasted opportunities. I was thankful that he and his adversary were mere figments of my imagination. Otherwise, I would be forced to introduce a whole new genre of stories to my friends behind the counter.

- - - - - - - - - - - - - - - - - - - -

I tried settling back into work but the woman in the skirt continued to crowd out every thought in my brain. I grabbed my cigarettes, thinking a quick smoke might help to clear my head. As I rose from my chair the Queen Fairy materialized again, this time in a throne atop my computer. The pink boa was draped over the center tip of his pitchfork.

"You blew a BIG opportunity," he scolded, twitching his index finger back and forth as he spoke. "Straight broads are every lesbian's fantasy, you know."

The Angel appeared beside him before I could offer a rebuttal.

"You again?" he scowled, slamming his makeshift staff against the monitor. "Will I ever be rid of you?"

"Not likely," the Angel snickered. "We are in this together, good buddy."

"I got your 'good buddy' right here, sister!" he ranted, wildly waving the tines in her direction.

"Calm down, Lewis. Remember what happened the last time you got yourself in a tizzy like this."

Directing his comments to the ceiling, he yelled, "Why is this woman always in my face? Can't I be partnered with someone else? She is the biggest 'you know what' on this entire task force!"

While I chuckled at their banter, a voice boomed out behind me, "What in the world are you laughing at, Dusty?"

I turned to see Beth standing in the doorway.

"Never mind," she said, shaking her head. "I'm sure I don't want to know."

I was shocked and relieved that she hadn't pressed me for an explanation. Instead, she folded her arms together and leaned against the doorjamb.

"That woman was freakin' gorgeous!" she squealed. "If I was a lesbian, I'd definitely be creaming my jeans right now." Winking, she added, "Who am I kidding? She was *soooo* goddamn hot I just might ask her out myself!"

I shoved my lighter in my pocket and moved to stand beside her.

"I need a favor," I said in a quieted voice. "Would you pull her file and…"

"Way ahead of you, Kemosabe. I got it while you were ogling her in the parking lot. Her name is Shane DuBois. She owns a place called 'The Bizarre Bazaar.'"

"I know the name of her company. I designed her letterhead, remember?"

"Oh yeah. Sorry."

"Is she with anyone? I mean, is she married?"

"How would I know? We don't put shit like that in our files. Your sex glands must be in high gear again." Going completely off-topic without so much as a segue, she added, "Are you taking anyone to the Christmas party this year? Last time you came alone and, let's be honest, you were a real Debbie Downer."

"Nice transition, Beth."

"As always. It's part of my charm. You are going, aren't you?"

"I'm planning on it. I don't have a date yet, but it's a little early to be worrying about that. The party is still two months away."

"You don't have a very good track record, my friend. You really should start now to find someone to go with you. It would definitely improve your odds if you let them know there's going to be free food and free booze, then you can pick the prettiest *or* the easiest, whichever is more appropriate."

"I hope I never have to stoop that low to get a date."

"We do what we must, Dusty. All is fair in love and lust."

"You are such a freak, Beth. Say, why don't *you* go with me?"

"Girl, I am way too much woman for you."

"Right," I replied smartly. "Now who's dreaming?"

—— A Chance Worth Taking ——

The woman from the bazaar returned to the store a few days later. I had gone home earlier in the day, so the following morning Beth shared with me all that had transpired.

"That woman was here yesterday," she announced when she saw me.

"What woman?"

"That bazaar woman."

"What bizarre woman? Are you saying some freak from my past showed up here at work? Oh my God. It was Tiffany, wasn't it?"

"Don't be an ass. You know who I'm talking about. The woman from the bazaar."

"Sorry I missed it."

"She was, too."

"What are you talking about?"

"She asked about you. Wanted to know if you were here."

"Are you fucking with me, Beth?"

"Nope. She wanted to pass along her appreciation for all that you've done for her."

"Okay. Now I know you're fucking with me. What did she really want?"

"She's getting compliments on the new logo and wanted to say thanks."

"Anything else?"

"Yeah, she put in an order for business cards with the new logo."

"Does she want the layout to stay the same? No other changes?"

"I'm assuming. She didn't say to change anything except the logo."

I didn't waste any time rummaging through my files and located the disk for that business card before Beth made it back to the lobby. After inserting it into the drive, I sat down and opened the file on my computer. As I stared at the screen, an idea came to mind.

She didn't ask for it, I thought to myself, *but I could really make this card pop with a new design. I'll just have Beth fax her the new layout when I'm finished.*

Thirty minutes later, I was handing Beth a printout with two different card designs.

"What is this?" she asked, staring at the paper.

"Some new ideas for the bazaar lady to look over. Would you fax this to her?"

"She didn't ask for a new design, Dusty."

"I know. But once I got started, I couldn't stop."

"You aren't by chance trying to win her over to the 'gay' side of the fence, are you?"

"No," I replied, blushing.

Beth laid the paper on the counter and tapped her finger on one of the designs.

"I like this one best," she said. "Adding the elephant was a good idea. Really cool."

"Let me know if she chooses one of these or wants to stay with the original."

"Sure. I'll send it right over. Wait… Maybe I should call her first since she wasn't expecting a design change."

I smiled, which prompted her to inquire, "Would *you* rather make the call?"

"No way! I wouldn't know what to say!"

"Good Lord, Dusty. It's not that difficult. You simply tell her you have some new layouts for her business card that you want her to take a look at. Then you ask her to let you know which, if either, she prefers."

"You go ahead. You know I'm not much of a people person."

"Since when? That's not the Dusty I know! I think you should be the one to call."

"That's your job, Beth. I'm just the wizard behind the curtain."

I returned to my office and waited for her to pick up the phone. When she did, I pressed my ear against the glass.

"Miss DuBois? This is Beth from Bob's Print Shop. Our graphic artist came up with some new ideas for your business card and I'd like to fax them over for you to look at. Is that okay?"

A brief silence was followed by, "Yes, ma'am. I have the number on file. You should be receiving them shortly. Call me back and let me know if you want to move forward with one of the new designs or stay with the old one."

Another short pause, then, "Sounds good. Thanks, Miss DuBois. Have a great day!"

- -

In less than twenty-four hours, Miss DuBois was back in the store.

"You didn't need to drive over here," Beth told her. "You could have just called with your decision."

"I'd like to speak with the artist," she responded. "I wanted to ask if she could make a change to one of the layouts."

"Oh, okay. I'll go get her."

Beth cleared her throat as she entered my office.

"Hey, Dusty. Your lady friend from the bazaar wants to talk to you."

Without turning around, I asked, "What line is she on?"

"She's not on the phone. She's out front."

Still staring at my computer, I answered with a giggle, "She's here?"

"Take it down a notch, Casanova. 'Desperate' doesn't look good on you."

My face immediately turned several different shades of red.

"Shut up, Beth," I muttered as I hurried around her.

Once in the lobby, I stepped behind the counter. Beth was right on my tail.

"Hi," I offered nervously. "Beth said you wanted to see me?"

"Yes. First off, thanks for the new designs. They are really spectacular!" Laying her faxed sheet on the counter, she pointed to one of the images and said, "I like this one best. The one with the elephant."

She looked up at me momentarily then returned her gaze to the paper.

"Is there any way you could jewel it up a bit?"

"I'm not sure what that means."

She reached into her purse and retrieved an old, black and white photograph and slid it across the counter toward me.

"This is my great-grandfather in Persia. See the bedazzled elephant behind him?"

I nodded my head slowly while studying the picture.

"Could you accessorize the elephant on the business card like that?"

"Shouldn't be that difficult. Do you want to wait for it? I'm working on another job right now but should be finished shortly."

"I'm meeting with a distributor this afternoon and need to get some things together beforehand. I could come back tomorrow."

"No need. I'll just have Beth fax you the new design."

"I don't mind. That way I'm here in case there are other changes to discuss." She then turned to Beth and asked, "Do I need to make an appointment?"

"That's not necessary," I answered for her. "Just come straight on back to my office when you get here."

She returned the next day at around the same time and, after Beth greeted her in the lobby, announced, "I'm here to see the artist."

"The artist?'" Beth echoed with a snorting laugh. "Around here, we keep things real and call her by name. Calling her 'the artist' inflates her ego too much."

Miss DuBois laughed in return before responding, "I only called her that because I have no idea what her name is."

"It's Dusty," Beth said. "Go on back. She's expecting you."

Miss DuBois moved past her and came directly to my office. Tapping lightly on the glass, she said, "I'm back!"

I stood up and motioned for her to enter.

"Is now a good time?" she asked.

"I just finished another project, so this is perfect timing. Come in and have a seat."

"In your chair? But where will you sit?"

"I don't mind standing. It's a nice change of pace every once in a while."

She seated herself and turned to face the computer. My arm brushed lightly against hers as I reached around her to insert the disk with her new design.

"Sorry," I muttered in a low voice. "I didn't mean to crowd you out."

"Do I need to move out of your way?"

"Only if this bothers you."

"Not at all. Do whatever you need to do."

Reaching around her a second time, I clicked the mouse and the new layout quickly filled the screen. A noise from behind gave us a start, causing both of us to turn around at the same time. There was Kathy, looming in the doorway.

"Is everything okay in here?" she asked. Her voice sounded angry.

"Everything is fine," Miss DuBois answered before turning back to the monitor.

Kathy gave me a glaring look and grumbled in a tone loud enough for only me to hear, "Behave yourself."

I offered a quick nod and waved my hand to shoo her away. After she left I turned back to my desk and grabbed the mouse again, purposely brushing my arm against Miss DuBois' to see what type of reaction it would provoke. My heart skipped a beat when she looked up at me and smiled.

Adding jewels to the elephant hadn't taken much effort and she seemed genuinely pleased with the changes. I printed her a copy of the new design and escorted her back to the lobby. Before leaving the store, she touched my arm and said, "Thank you, Dusty. This really meant a lot to me."

Beth and Maggie both came into my office numerous times that afternoon, teasing me incessantly about the goofy look I had on my face when Miss DuBois was in my chair and the flush in my cheeks when she left. Knowing it was the truth, I had no choice but to agree with them.

━ ━ ━ ━ ━ ━ ━ ━ ━ ━ ━ ━ ━ ━ ━ ━ ━ ━ ━ ━

Later that afternoon Beth and I were discussing a new club that had just opened in Dallas and since she and Dan were no longer together (he refused her proposal), I invited her to go with me to check it out. She said no at first but then gave in when I offered to pay for her drinks.

"Just so you know," she said. "I plan on getting soused."

"Fine by me," I told her. "There's only thirty bucks on that tab so you better choose your drinks wisely."

"What a cheap date you are!"

"C'mon, Beth. You know I'm saving my money in case I meet 'Miss Right.'"

"And just who am I?"

"You would be 'Miss Right Now.' There's a big difference."

"Screw you, Dusty. Just for that, I will not be dancing with you tonight."

"In all the times we've gone out, you've never once danced with me."

"Yeah, well... I might have considered it, but you just killed any chance of that!"

"I'm only interested in seeing what kind of music they play and whether or not any of my people are there."

"Your people. You make it sound like you're from another planet."

"We are. We're from the planet Lesbos, remember?"

"Your lesbian sisters, maybe. I think you're from Uranus."

"Ha, ha. Very funny."

"So, what time are you picking me up?"

"Who said I was driving?"

"I told you I plan to get wasted so you have to drive. You wouldn't want me to cause an accident, would you?"

"No. Especially since that would put me in the passenger seat. I'll pick you up at nine thirty. Don't keep me waiting like you did the last time."

"I'm always worth the wait, my friend."

"Maybe if I had a penis."

"You probably don't know this, but there are such things as mechanical penises."

"Nope. Didn't know that. Probably could have gone the rest of my life without knowing it, too."

She flipped me the bird then turned and walked away.

"Be on time," I called out after her.

— — — — — — — — — — — — — — — — — — — —

I pulled up to Beth's house at nine thirty, and, as usual, she kept me waiting in the car for another fifteen minutes. To make up for her lateness, she promised not to spend the entire bar tab that night. As we were walking to the club from the parking lot, she told me she was on the hunt for a new man. I didn't want any part of that, so we decided to go our separate ways once we were inside.

"Meet me here at closing time," she told me before disappearing into the crowd.

I made my way to the bar and fell in line behind other patrons waiting to be served. When I reached the counter, the bartender, an androgynous-looking woman in a pair of overalls with a sports bra underneath smiled and asked me, "What can I get you, sweetie?"

"What do you have on tap?"

She rattled off a bunch of brands, most of which I didn't catch.

"I'll have a Bud Light," I said when she had finished.

"We don't have that on tap. Only in the bottle."

"I'm good with that."

After popping off the cap, she draped the bottle in a napkin and handed it to me.

"That'll be three bucks."

I pulled a five-dollar bill from my pocket and set it on the counter.

"Keep the change," I told her.

The smile she offered in return let me know we would be on friendly terms for the remainder of the evening. I took a swig of beer as I approached the dance floor and slipped into an empty spot to claim it for myself. I was only there a few moments when someone tapped me on the shoulder.

"Hey you!" a voice shouted in my ear.

I turned around and locked eyes with the woman from the bazaar.

"Hello, Miss Dubois," I answered. "How are you?"

"Call me Shane," she responded. "I'm doing well! I'm here with a friend and was just on my way to the bar. Can I get you anything?"

I flashed my bottle of Bud and shook my head no.

"Okay then. Hopefully we'll cross paths again at some point tonight."

I smiled and nodded. Seconds later, Beth assumed the space that she had vacated.

"You and the bazaar lady, huh?" she snickered. "Guess you've lined up your date for the evening."

"Don't be silly, Beth."

"Hey, listen," she said, nudging me with her elbow. "I'm gonna cut out pretty soon, so I won't be needing a ride home. I'm going to a private party, if you catch my meaning."

Looking past her, I saw a handsome man staring in our direction.

"Got it. See you at work on Monday. Be safe!"

"Thanks, Mom. I'll do my best. If not, I'll be sure to name it after you!"

She planted a peck on my cheek and was gone. I thought about leaving as well but then decided to have another drink first. I finished the bottle I was holding and tossed it into the trash on the way to the bar. When I got close enough, I saw that Shane had made it halfway through the service line. Knowing it would be rude to cut in, I handed her some cash and asked her to get my drink with hers then stood against the back wall and waited for her to bring it to me.

"My friend is out on the dance floor," she said after handing me my beer. "Mind if I hang out with you until she comes back?"

"Sure!" I answered in a voice that was a full octave higher than normal. It seemed to echo a cheerleader's cry after the winning touchdown at a high school football game. The very sound of it made me shudder.

"Are you here with anyone?" she asked.

"I came with one of my coworkers but she got a better offer and is on her way out the door as we speak."

"Well, that sucks."

"It's all right. I'm having fun watching everyone dance."

"Do you like to dance?"

"No, but I like to watch."

Wrong thing to say, moron, I scolded myself. *Now she probably thinks I'm some kind of pervert.*

"I like to watch, too," she confessed.

Thank you, God...

Unfortunately, our conversation ended before it had a chance to start as her friend showed up to steal her away. Pointing at me, the friend asked, "Who's this?"

"This is Dusty," Shane told her.

"Hello," the friend said. "Dusty... What a freaking awesome name that is!" She then turned to Shane and asked, "Have you found a man yet?"

A scowl came over her Shane's face as she retaliated, "You have absolutely no couth whatsoever, Sandra."

"I get no respect for trying to help a sister out," Sandra whined. "It's time to get you back on the market, girl! It's been a really long time since..."

"Don't go any further with that," Shane interrupted. "Dusty doesn't need to hear how long it's been."

"Just sayin' that it's time, Shane," Sandra countered. "You need to get busy before those spinster tendencies of yours become irreversible!

Besides, I hear that your hoo-haw closes up if you don't use it. Kinda like pierced ears."

"Ha!" Shane snorted, then, a second later, exclaimed, "Wait… That's not funny!"

All three of us burst into laughter simultaneously. My attraction to Shane seemed to grow exponentially at that moment and I knew I would probably end up doing or saying something regretful if I was around her much longer. When my second beer was finished, I thanked them for the company then excused myself to go home.

—— MERRY CHRISTMAS, DARLING ——

I wanted to go back to the club a few weeks later in hopes I might see Shane again, but the guy Beth picked up turned out to be a keeper so she didn't want to go out anymore. Crowds always made me uncomfortable; there was no way I would go by myself. I thought about asking Kathy or Maggie but quickly vetoed that idea. I liked them at work, but, at a bar? Probably not so much. And besides, what did I think would happen if I did run into Shane? That she would magically become a lesbian just for me? Surely, I could find a real lesbian to go out with. Unfortunately, that didn't happen in time for the Christmas party.

- -

Bob closed the store early on the day of the party so that everyone would have time to go home and get ready. At seven o'clock his car pulled in beside mine and Angela, his wife, raced over to greet me. She and I always had fun at the office parties, mainly because we were both obnoxiously competitive and would spend the entire night trying to one up each other. At every party she challenged me to a drink-off, though I don't know why she bothered. She was a lightweight who could never make it past four rounds at most. Bob, on the other hand, could drink me under the table. There isn't a time at any of our outings that I recall seeing his glass anywhere near empty.

We had been there about an hour when Angela dared me to a duel of Tequila shots. I hadn't eaten all day, planning to save room for the exorbitant amount of food Bob always had catered at these shindigs.

Plus, I wanted to pace myself to avoid becoming intoxicated too early. But, being prideful, I couldn't let her walk away with an easy win.

I had just put away my second Margarita when she made the challenge but figured it wasn't enough to hinder the competition. Bob purchased an entire bottle of Tequila and set it on the bar in front of us and we were tied at four shots apiece when Angela slammed back a fifth. I was impressed she had made it that far but knew she wouldn't last to six. I sucked down two in a row before hammering my glass on the counter. She raised hers to her lips but quickly put it back down and waved her hand to signal defeat.

The walls were spinning as I scanned the room for my coworkers and I literally had to keep one eye closed to prevent multiple faces from looking back at me. I knew then that I would be staying on the wagon for the remainder of the evening.

Beth and her new beau, Tom, had carpooled with Maggie and her husband, Paul, who volunteered to be the designated driver for the ride home. Kathy came alone because her boyfriend, Steve, was playing a gig that night with his band. Knowing where everyone would be heading next, the five of them left before the contest ended and went to find empty seats near the pool table. Me and Angela, still carrying what was left in the Tequila bottle, staggered in not long after with Bob in close pursuit.

I placed a stack of quarters on the rail before sitting down, knowing at some point I would have to play a game of Snooker with Bob. It was no secret that everyone let him win because the longer he played (and won), the longer the party (and his tab) would last. The irony in that was hysterical, considering what a tight-ass he usually was when it came to money.

Bob was far from sober when it came our turn to play. I saw a line of spittle trailing from his mouth to the felt as he lowered his head to line up one of his shots, which in turn caused me to laugh so hard that I nearly wet myself. I handed my cue stick to Paul to fill in for me and hurried to the ladies' room.

The sounds of drunken women filled the air as I stood in line waiting for an open stall. Some were staring, which was commonplace for me. I'm very flat-chested, so I never wear a bra. I don't wear makeup, either. To top things off, all of those years in the military put me in the habit of keeping my hair relatively short. I'm sure everyone standing around wondered if I was a confused young man who had accidentally staggered into their den of estrogen by mistake.

Finally, a stall door opened and I stepped forward, thankful that it was my turn. I peed for an incredibly long time then remained seated to burn a cigarette. After smoking it down to the filter, I flicked the butt into the toilet and swung open the door. I'm not sure exactly how long I was in there, but the crowd was gone and the room had grown quiet. I felt much better though, not nearly as inebriated as when I first arrived.

I reached for the exit door at the same time someone was pushing in from the other side. Stepping back, I held it open for their entry. A blast of heat shot through my crotch as Shane DuBois crossed in front of me.

"Merry Christmas," she offered in passing.

She took another step forward then stopped and slowly turned to face me.

"Dusty!" she squealed after realizing it was me. "What are you doing here?"

Before I could answer, she stepped forward and folded her arms around my neck. The smell of alcohol on her breath was strong and, although I had consumed more than the legal limit myself, we were likely on par with one another as far as level of intoxication.

"Are you here alone?" she asked.

I didn't know which question to answer first so I put more emphasis on the latter, hoping she might be inclined to change my solitary status.

"It's our office Christmas party but yeah, I'm here alone."

Taking my hand in hers, she said, "What a pity. Someone as cute as you shouldn't be at a party all by yourself!"

My heart stopped beating momentarily then resounded with a thunderous clap. I was convinced she heard it. Hell, given how loud it was, I was sure everyone in the club heard it, too.

I glanced toward the mirror trusting the Queen Fairy would be there to impart his infamous words of encouragement. His usual spot was deserted; no pitchfork or boa in sight. I hesitated to seek out the Angel, fearing that furrowed brow of hers might dampen my enthusiasm. After taking a deep breath, I dared myself to look at the opposite shoulder and what I saw sent waves of shock through my system. The Angel was there with a band of duct tape over her mouth and her wrists bound together with the Queen Fairy's feathery sash. Lewis was standing behind her with one hand on his hip and the other triumphantly snapping out a big letter "Z." He offered me a quick wink and blew a kiss in my direction.

"Isn't it crazy that we just happened to randomly run into each other again?" Shane asked. "This is twice we've been at the same bar at the exact same time!"

"Yeah. It is a little crazy. Who would've thought, right? Maybe it's fate."

"Maybe so. Maybe we are exactly where we're supposed to be."

"So, are you here with someone?" I asked hesitantly.

"I'm here with my brother, Michael, and his girlfriend. It's her office party tonight and they invited me to tag along. What a coincidence, huh?"

I let out an audible sigh of relief after hearing that she had not come with a date of her own. "Yeah," I muttered. "What are the odds in that happening?"

Our hands drifted apart and a long, uncomfortable pause settled between us. The silence was stifling. I knew it was time to go.

"I should probably get back to the party now. It was nice seeing you again, Shane."

"Before you go," she announced anxiously, "there is something I want to ask you."

"Sure. Okay."

"This is probably out of line, but…" She hesitated, eyeing me with an odd sort of fascination and then brazenly inquired, "Are you gay?"

My jaw dropped and a blank stare came over my face.

"You don't have to tell me if you don't want to. I know it's none of my business. I was just curious."

"Would my answer make a difference?"

"I don't think so. No, I'm sure it wouldn't."

"Tell her," the Queen Fairy urged. Feeling a sudden pain in my earlobe, I shifted my eyes to the mirror and caught him sinking his teeth into my flesh. "TELL HER!" he shouted.

"Yes," I replied, wincing. "I'm a lesbian."

"I thought so. I don't know any gay people but you seem really nice."

"Thanks, but I don't think the two are necessarily related. Why would you want to know if I'm gay?"

"My friend, Sandra, brought it up after you left us at the other bar."

"Well, now you can tell her and solve the mystery."

Color flushed my cheeks as I shifted my weight nervously from one leg to the other and shoved my hands into my pockets. Shane sensed that I was uncomfortable and added another little morsel which immediately put me at ease.

"Hey, I don't care if you're gay or not," she avowed with firm conviction. "I like you and that's all that matters."

"Thanks. Listen, it's been great talking with you, but I should probably go. I've been gone a long time and I'm sure my coworkers are wondering where I've disappeared to."

"I hope I haven't upset you."

"Not at all."

She smiled a broad, wide smile, which I returned with one of my own.

"Good," she responded, then added, "Can I give you another hug before you go?"

Once again, she came forward before I could say anything and latched her arms around me. I felt her warm breath in my ear as her head came in contact with my shoulder.

Holding me tightly, she whispered, "Do you really have to go?"

I backed away from her and held out my hands to keep us arm's length apart.

"Look, Shane. I'm not sure where you're going with this…"

"I know I'm here with my brother and his girlfriend, but it's kinda lonely hanging out with them. I'd rather be with you tonight."

"Shane…"

"Please? You've been on my mind a lot lately and I'd really like for you to stay."

"Go for it," the Queen Fairy urged. "Do it. You know you want to. She's offering, so why not?"

I sensed that resistance would be a winless fight because my brain was screaming "No!" while my head was nodding "Yes!"

After leading me into a stall, Shane latched the door behind us. Her lips landed on mine while she tugged at her blouse, struggling to free it from the confines of her skirt. When it was completely out, she pushed my hand up under the material and placed it over her breast.

With no regard for getting caught, I reached behind her and unfastened her bra, then slowly opened the buttons on her shirt, pausing just long enough to kiss the newly exposed flesh behind each one.

Placing my hands on her waist I pulled her close, her stance widening as my thigh came to rest against her pubic bone. Heat immediately began to radiate through my jeans and onto my leg.

"Take this off," she panted while pulling on my shirt to lift it over my head.

Eager to oblige, it quickly went sailing over our heads and onto the floor beside the commode. Her bra and blouse were next and she let out a soft moan as I guided them over her shoulders. At the same time, I felt another surge of hot steam on my thigh.

"Touch me," she pleaded. "Touch me now!"

She pulled her skirt up around her waist while I positioned my hand between her legs. When my fingers brushed against her thigh she reared back on her heels and nearly lost her balance so I backed up to the toilet, bringing her with me as I sat down. My mouth then searched hungrily for her nipple while my hands moved to their rightful places: the left one on the small of her back, the right one immersed in the hot pool she had prepared for me. I massaged her clit, lightly at first then harder as her movements intensified. Her thigh muscles tightened and her fingernails dug deep into my back as her orgasm reached its climax.

She slumped forward afterwards and blurted out, "*Jesus!*"

"I have been called a lot of things," I said, "but never..."

She placed her lips over mine in an obvious attempt to silence me. As her tongue struggled to win control over mine, her hips began to gyrate back and forth once again. I slid two fingers into her vagina and felt the wall muscles clamp around them, sealing them inside. Her nails blazed a new trail across my shoulders as her body shuddered through a second orgasm.

We shared a slow, passionate kiss before she climbed off of my lap. Her legs were wobbly as she tried to straighten her skirt, which had bound itself up around her waist. I leaned over to collect our tops, only to have her snatch them from me and toss them back onto the floor.

"Not so fast," she purred. "It's my turn."

My nipples immediately hardened as if some invisible commander had just called them to attention. Backing me into the wall, she drove my hands high above my head with one of her own. Her other hand quickly maneuvered its way inside of my jeans, her long fingers gliding easily through the wetness and filling me completely. Shortly after, an explosion occurred beneath her powerful fingertips.

Exhausted, we stood in each other's embrace. When we finally parted, she gave me a peck on the cheek, which caused my nipples to harden all over again. Her mouth quickly settled over one of them while she gently massaged the other.

"Stop!" I pleaded. "I won't be able to walk if we do it again."

She took a step back and said in a low voice, "Perhaps we could meet again…"

Her voice trailed off; the remainder of her statement abandoned. The implication was clear, however, so I nodded my affirmation. I then stooped over to gather our clothes, giving her a clear view of the marks on my back.

"Oh my God!" she gasped. "Are you all right?"

"I'm good, actually."

"I can't believe I did that to you! I'm so sorry!"

"There is nothing to be sorry about, Shane. It's just a few scratches."

She moved behind me and kissed the top of my shoulder, just above the wounds, and whispered in my ear, "I've never done this sort of thing before."

"You aren't sorry it happened, are you?"

"No. Are you?"

"Not at all. To be honest, I'd love to stay in here with you all night. But this is Texas, after all, and we should probably leave before they send someone to arrest us. They don't take too kindly to this… ummm… thing that we…"

"Please don't finish that sentence."

She stepped away to fasten her bra and button her blouse, returning that pair of magnificent breasts to their secret hiding place. Afterwards she helped me with my shirt, carefully lifting it over the scratches on my back.

We shared one last kiss before parting and then I waited until she left the restroom before coming out of the stall. Glancing in the mirror, I saw that the Queen Fairy and the Angel were still together on the same shoulder. The Angel's bindings were gone. So, too, was her off-putting scowl.

I placed my hand between them and Lewis latched onto my little finger as though he were clinging to it for dear life. Grateful for all he had done to accommodate my time with Shane, I carefully transported him back to his rightful abode.

My coworkers talked nonstop about the party when we went back to work. During Christmas and New Year holidays business was excruciatingly slow, affording them even more time than usual to chatter back and forth. I made it a point to purposely avoid their conversations, hoping to deflect any possibility of self-incrimination. It was for naught as Beth noticed my absence and went out of her way to put me on the spot.

"What's going on with you, Dusty?" she asked. "You don't seem like yourself today."

"I just have a lot on my mind."

"We never saw you again after the Snooker game. Did you go home after that?"

"I was in the bathroom. By the time I came out you were all gone."

"Wow. You were in there an awfully long time then. Were you sick?"

"Uh, no."

"That lady from the bazaar was there. Her name slips my mind for some reason. Anyways… Did you see her?"

"Her name is Shane, and yes, I saw her. Quite a lot of her, actually."

"Biblically?"

"In a manner of speaking."

"Why you little slut puppy! Adding to your collection of hot lesbian stories, are you? I can't wait to hear this one. I have work to do but I will be back. Don't you dare leave this room! Promise?"

"I promise. But don't say anything to Kathy, okay? You know how she gets."

"No worries. I will carry this to my grave."

An hour or so later, Beth returned as promised.

"Are you going to see her again?" she asked, picking up right where she'd left off.

"I don't know," I mumbled. "Maybe. I would like to…"

Maggie burst into the room before I could finish.

"I took a call from Shane DuBois a little while ago," she said excitedly. "She wanted to speak with you, Dusty, but you were on another line. She asked for your home phone number so I gave it to her. Was that all right? Beth told me you two were an item now."

I looked at Beth and frowned. "To the grave, huh?"

"Hey," she replied defensively. "You said not to tell Kathy. You never said anything about Maggie."

Just then, Kathy came to the door pushing her way past the two of them. Her face was scrunched into a scowl.

"Maggie told me you had sex with one of our customers at the party, Dusty. I can't believe you did that! Man, I sure hope she doesn't sue us over this."

"Sue us?" Beth echoed. "For what? Bad sex? Or, uh... uh... premature ejaculation? Wait... Do lesbians ejaculate?"

"Hey!" I shouted angrily. "I am still in the room!"

"I can't believe you told Maggie," I added, my eyes now fixed on Beth.

She stared at the floor, unable to return my gaze. I transferred my glare to Maggie, who quickly responded in like fashion. Bob strolled past shortly after and reminded us we were paid to work, not to gab. It was nearly quitting time anyways, so I bid farewell to my nosy coworkers and drove home as quickly as possible, anxious not to miss Shane's call.

Hurrying inside, I snatched the phone from the living room and carried it into the bedroom. I stared at it the entire time I was changing my clothes, impatiently waiting and wishing it would ring. When it did, I hesitated to pick it up, fearing the cheerleader who commandeered my voice that night at the first bar might return for a repeat performance. I decided not to say anything, opting to let the caller speak first instead. After pushing the Talk button, I brought the phone up to my ear.

"Hello?" a voice beckoned from the other end of the line.

A couple more seconds passed and then, "H-e-l-l-o?" they repeated, this time a bit more demanding. "Is anyone there? Dusty?"

"Yeah," I grumbled, realizing it wasn't Shane. The caller was my friend, Marge.

"Why didn't you say anything?"

"I wanted you to go first."

"Why?"

"Because I wanted to know who it was before I said anything."

"Again, I ask... Why?"

"Remember me telling you about the woman from the store?"

"The one in the skirt?"

"Yeah. She's supposed to be calling."

"Back it up, sister. How did you go from carrying boxes to her car to a phone call?"

"I sort of ran into her at our office party last Friday and we did the wild thing in the restroom."

"For real? No fucking way! How did that happen? Start talking, girlfriend. Fill me in and don't skip a thing. Give me all the details."

When my story was finished, Marge screamed into the phone, "You are one damn lucky bitch, you know it? That shit only happens in porn flicks or in one of those cheap lesbian novels. Are you telling me the truth, Dusty? Swear it?"

"It's the truth, Marge. I swear. I even have the claw marks to prove it."

"I'm gonna want to check those out. So, tell me about her. Does she have a sister?"

"Honestly, Marge, I don't know that much about her. I'm not even sure she's gay."

"Dusty, dear, this woman does the hokey pokey with you in a public restroom and you don't know if she is gay? Let me slap you on the head, honey. Straight women don't go around fucking lesbians in the potty."

She did have a point. Maybe Shane was a lesbian who hadn't been brave enough to come out of the closet. Still…

"I'm going to that new bar tonight," Marge said, interrupting my thoughts. "Wanna come with me?"

"No thanks. It's nice, though. I think you'll like it. I know I did."

"Tell me one thing you remember about that bar – besides the lady in the skirt."

"Very funny, Marge."

"You are such a putz, my friend. Okay. I'll call you later in the week."

I walked to the kitchen and set the phone on the table then quickly picked it up and tucked it under my arm while I rummaged through the fridge for a cold pop. No sooner than I sat down to drink it I felt the urge to pee, so I carried both with me to the bathroom. I had just finished emptying my bladder when the phone rang again. I assumed it would be Marge calling back with more questions, but this time it was another friend, Biff.

I had met Marge and Biff the year before while singing in an all-lesbian chorus and we became instant friends. We had so much fun at rehearsals that we decided to chum around outside of chorus as well.

Marge has always been a carefree, "say it like she means it" kind of gal, while Biff, the Brainiac, weighed her thoughts before responding. Two more polar opposites you will never find. I'm more "middle-of-the-road," easily agreeable with either personality. The three of us blended perfectly.

Marge was the tallest of our trio, standing about 5' 10" in her stocking feet. Biff was maybe 5' 7", while I barely hit the 5' 2" mark. I was definitely the runt of the litter. Marge was fiercely protective of me and would challenge anyone she considered a threat to my well-being, emotionally or physically. Biff was more like an older sister, even though she was the youngest of our group. She always had sage advice, which I took to heart whenever it was offered. Marge followed the beat of her own drum whether it coincided with Biff's advice or not. Together, we were quite the menagerie.

Knowing Biff as I did, I readied myself for the inquisition that was sure to follow.

"I hear you've been steaming up some bathroom mirrors lately."

"Let me guess. You've been talking to Marge."

"You know that woman can't keep a secret. She called me right after hanging up with you. What is going on, Dusty? She told me you had sex with a stranger at your office party."

"Yeah, that's partly true. What she purposely left out is that she wasn't a stranger. I had met her before. At the store."

"And you had sex with her then, too? What kind of business is Bob running?"

The image of Biff pushing her glasses up the bridge of her nose suddenly popped into my head. And, in that same image, I could see her eyes rolling behind the lenses.

"Don't be ridiculous, Biff. You know what kind of business it is."

"So how did the two of you end up in a public toilet, Dusty? Were you drunk?"

"We had both been drinking, but not together. I was there for my office party. We just happened to run into each other in the bathroom."

"That's the most literal thing you've said so far. Marge was right, this does sound pretty farfetched. Are you planning to see her again?"

"I don't know. Maggie gave her my number so now I'm just waiting for her to call."

"Good ol' Maggie, clueless as ever. Not a thought in her head she may have given your number to a psychopath."

"You know what they say, 'crazy in the head, crazy in the bed.'"

"Yeah, well tell that to a psychiatrist. You need to be careful, Dusty. She sounds like a wolf in sheep's clothing."

"You worry too much, Biff. I'll be fine."

"I will always worry about you. You're my friend."

"Thanks. Oops, gotta go. I have another call coming in. It might be her."

I switched over to the new call, cutting Biff off halfway through her goodbye.

"Hello?" I announced as I brought the phone to my ear. Pressing it firmly against my earlobe, I listened but heard nothing.

"Hello? Shane? Is that you?"

I waited a few moments but only silence followed, so I placed the receiver back on the charger. I plopped down into my recliner, thinking it would only be a short wait until Shane called. The hours passed slowly with everyone I knew ringing in. Everyone, that is, except her. When the clock struck twelve, I gave up the vigil; however, sleep did not come easily. I laid in bed for hours until fatigue finally directed my body to shut down.

—— ALONE AGAIN, NATURALLY ——

Days turned into weeks without a single call from Shane. During one of my many temper tantrums of late, instigated by her dismissal and the fact I was about to celebrate another birthday alone, I decided to get shit-faced drunk and drown my woes in a bottle of Tequila. I invited Biff and Marge to share in my misery (masqueraded as my birthday), to which both answered with an enthusiastic "YES!" I also invited Butch, a nickname given to another of our friends (for obvious reasons), but, as usual, she was pulling a double and had to work.

I was desperate to ease the pain of Shane's rejection. I really liked her and thought she liked me as well. My heart was hurting, reminiscent of the feelings I had as a teenager during the long U-Haul ride from Missouri to Texas. I needed reassurance, even if it was for only one night in the arms of someone new. The way it played out didn't matter to me. And I knew it wouldn't matter to Shane, either.

Standing in front of the dresser, I twisted the lid off of my favorite cologne and put a smidge behind each ear, then splashed a little along the sides of my face and the back of my neck. And, as further enticement to anyone showing even the slightest bit of interest, I dabbed a little between my breasts, too. Just in case.

I wore this same cologne back in the tournament days, I reminded myself. *It sure worked its magic back then. And, though I hate to admit it, at the office party, too. I hope it packs that same kind of punch tonight!*

I squeezed into a tight pair of jeans and topped them with a form-fitting shirt then grabbed my keys and darted out the door. Biff was waiting at the curb with the top down in her brand new, cherry red Chevy Cavalier.

"When did you buy this?" I asked as I settled into the passenger seat.

"Yesterday. It suits me, don't you think?"

"Yes, it does. Almost matches your hair color."

Feigning a smile, she quickly moved on to her next topic.

"Did the skirt lady ever call?"

"Well, hello to you, too, Biff. Don't you look nice tonight."

"Forget the small talk, Dusty. I asked you a question."

"No. She never called."

"Better you found out sooner than later. You don't need that kind of drama."

"I guess. It still hurts, though. You know what? Let's not talk about her tonight."

"Got it. My lips are sealed."

Biff took her pledge to heart and we sat in relative silence until Marge strolled into the bar a few minutes after us. Draping an arm over my shoulder, her first question to me was, "How's your back?" immediately followed by, "Any new claw marks?"

I looked up from my Margarita and stared into the eyes of my silver-haired friend.

"It's fine," I grumbled.

Seeing that Biff and I already had our drinks, Marge ordered herself a beer.

"Did the wild woman ever…?" she started to ask but then Biff shook her head to cut her off.

"Screw her," Marge said. "You're better off without her, Dusty."

"I don't want to talk about Shane tonight," I told both of them. "In fact, I would like to pretend that she never existed."

"Not a problem. We can do that for our dear friend, can't we, Biff?"

Biff didn't answer. Her attention had been diverted to the other side of the bar.

"There's a hottie over there waving at me," she announced. "I don't know who this person is, but she is drop-dead gorgeous!"

Marge and I craned our necks in the direction of Biff's finger. It only took a second for me to recognize the woman and I turned back to the bar as quickly as possible. Marge's beer was within reach, so I grabbed it and drank what was left in one swift motion.

"Hey!" she snapped. "That was *my* beer!"

I took a deep breath and muttered in a low voice, "That's her. That's Shane."

"No shit? What the hell is she doing here?"

Biff, always the realist, replied smugly, "Looks like dancing to me."

"Smartass," Marge growled. "I see that. I'm just surprised that she's here."

Biff then pointed out, "She definitely has her eye on you, Dusty."

I stole a glance in Shane's direction and saw that Biff was right, she *was* staring at me. When she waved again, the hairs on my arms stood on end under a blanket of goose bumps. I didn't return the gesture, knowing full well that martyrdom would be mine for the taking that night.

Marge suggested that we dance to show Shane I was with friends and not the least bit interested in what she had to offer, so we made our way to an open spot on the floor. Halfway through the song, a pair of unfamiliar hands appeared on my hips. Figuring they were Shane's I kept dancing, still hell bent on ignoring her. The hands then began twisting and turning my hips in ways that convinced me their owner wanted to have sex with me right where I stood. I looked at Biff and Marge. Both had the same confused expression on their faces.

The hands then crept toward my breasts and a sexy, female voice whispered in my ear, "Are you here alone?"

"Let's hope," I answered, nearly choking on my response. "Why do you ask?"

"I don't want any trouble," the voice replied.

All of a sudden, the person behind me grabbed one of my hands and directed it to a place inside of their clothing where hair, heat and moisture coexist. It was a bold gesture, I thought, even for Shane. I pulled away and turned around to explain that I wasn't that kind of girl, but froze when I found myself staring into the eyes of a total stranger. I wanted to run but was unable to move, my feet obviously hearing a different signal than the one my brain was trying to send.

Mistaking peril for lust, the woman gripped my ass and started gyrating her hips into mine. Marge stepped in at that point and pulled her off of me. Un-phased, the woman moved on to her next conquest while we hurried back to the bar. I was relieved she hadn't followed us. So were my friends.

"Who was that?" Biff asked.

"I have no idea," I answered honestly.

"Apparently that shit happens to Dusty all the time," Marge smirked as she flagged the bartender down to bring another round. "You know, wild, horny women just throwing themselves at her."

Something seemed to startle Biff and I saw her eyes open wide as if she were seeing a ghost. Immediately after, I felt the weight of someone leaning into my back.

"Nice show," a new voice growled in my ear. "Why did you stop? Why didn't you just fuck that woman right there on the dance floor?"

A different pair of hands spun me around, bringing me face to face with Shane.

"I thought you were a decent person," she said, then contradicted that by adding, "Obviously, I was mistaken."

"How can you say that?" I objected in my own defense.

I reached out to touch her arm and she reared back on her heels, roaring, "Don't touch me! *Don't ever fucking touch me again!*"

And with that, she stormed away. I quickly set out after her.

"Dusty!" Marge yelled. "Come back! She's not worth it!"

Ignoring my friend's warning I raced for the exit, hoping to catch Shane before she left the building. But it was too late. She had already made her way outside.

"I'll be right back," I said in passing to the girl checking IDs and collecting cover charges at the door.

"Excuse me," she replied defiantly. "You'll need a stamp to get back in."

I turned and waited, hand extended, as she rummaged through a large box stashed under the counter.

"Bear with me a sec," she said. "I know it's in here somewhere."

As if she had all the time in the world to find her stamping equipment, I grabbed a pen and hastily scribbled an "X" on my palm.

"There," I said, waving my hand in front of her face. "This will have to do. Can't you see I'm in a hurry?"

I burst through the doors and onto the sidewalk and saw right away that Shane had already made her way to the other side of the street. Oblivious to oncoming traffic, I darted out after her. An old man in a Nissan hatchback slammed on his brakes and began yelling obscenities, to which I apologized profusely and repeatedly while continuing to scurry across the remaining lanes.

"Shane!" I shouted after her. "Wait! Let me explain!"

Her stride quickened.

"Damn it, Shane. *STOP!*"

Running full speed, I caught up with her under a street lamp and grabbed her arm, forcing her to stop.

"Shane, you have to listen to me."

"Why? What is there to say?"

"You have no right to be angry with me. I *am* a nice person and really don't give a fat, flying fuck what you think of me. I have been waiting for weeks to hear from you. Why haven't you called?"

"I don't… I'm not…"

"Save it. I guess it's useless to tell you I have never seen that woman before. I don't know why she picked me to hit on. Maybe she thought I was cute. I really don't see how it's any of your business anyway. You haven't shown the slightest bit of interest in me since the night of the office party, so why shouldn't someone else? From now on you can keep your smartass opinions to yourself. You don't know me well enough to judge me."

I stared at her and she stared back. I couldn't tell if she believed me and, frankly, I was too mad to give a shit.

"You're right," she said, her angry glare starting to soften. "I don't know you. I tried to call but chickened out every time I picked up the phone. What happened between us was incredible, Dusty, but I was afraid to admit I was attracted to another woman. When I saw you tonight those feelings stirred up again, but your behavior on the dance floor has forced me to reconsider. I find it hard to believe you didn't know that woman. You didn't even try to stop her!"

"I'm telling you the truth, Shane. I have never seen that woman before. The reason I didn't stop her is because I thought it was you."

"And does that happen to you often? Strange women coming on to you like that, without provocation?"

"Weren't you a stranger when you came on to me?"

I didn't give her a chance to say anything more. I stepped past her and hurried to rejoin my friends at the bar.

- -

Since that fateful night I had come to the conclusion that Shane was more trouble than she was worth. Given the chance, I knew she would rip my heart to shreds. Biff and Marge were wet blankets whenever her name came up, so I called Butch to boohoo on her shoulder instead. She wasn't the least bit interested in what I had to say either.

"I met someone a few nights ago," she confided. "The feelings I have for this woman are really intense, Dusty. Way stronger than anyone else I've ever dated."

"Really? Wasn't it just last week you were gaga over some girl from that thug bar you go to?"

"This one's for real, Dusty. I feel it all the way down to my toenails."

"Not a pretty image, Butch. I've seen your toenails."

"Sorry, I can't talk now. I'm supposed to call her before she goes to work. I'll give you a shout later, okay?"

"All right. Take care."

"Same to you. Bye."

For weeks my emotions had been operating in overdrive, catapulting me from high to low several times a day. It was exhausting. Something had to change. But what? I tossed the phone back and forth in my hands while contemplating who else I could call to give me the answers I was so in need of. And then it hit me. I didn't need anyone else to help me make a change. *I* was the thing that needed to change.

I dialed the number for my hairdresser, convinced that a new look would dissociate me from the morbid, depressed creature I had become. Plus, I needed someone to talk to. People often bared their souls to their stylists and, on more than one occasion, I did, too. Rita had been cutting my hair for nearly a decade and I could tell her anything. Her advice to me all of those years had always been freely given and graciously accepted. Thankfully, she answered on the first ring and told me to come right over.

I entered the salon and slumped into her chair.

"What'll it be?" she asked as she pumped the foot pedal to raise my seat higher.

Her question reminded me of Mabel asking if I wanted meatloaf or chicken in that it meant I had a choice of haircuts from the menu. Locking eyes with my pitiful reflection, I told her, "Let's go crazy and do something new, Rita. Something that's totally opposite from this 'girl next door' thing I have going on now."

I turned my head in the direction of a new customer entering the salon and saw a poster of a woman with a short, punky haircut on the wall next to the door. Pointing to it, I said, "I want to look like the woman in that picture."

"Hmmm," Rita mumbled, gazing at the poster while stroking her chin. "Nah. That wouldn't look good on you. How about a pixie cut? You know, like Dorothy Hamill. Now that would be cute."

"My mother forced me to wear my hair like that as a teenager. I was Dorothy's clone for years. Those days are gone. I prefer to choose my own style now, thank you."

"Then choose something more reasonable, Dusty."

"Come on, Rita. Help me. I need a look that says I'm untamable, unreachable and untouchable. A look that epitomizes power, strength and purpose. Can you do that? Can you make me look like that?"

Placing her hands on her hips, Rita stepped back and gave me the once over.

"All that in a haircut? That's really funny, Dusty. Maybe if I had a magic wand…"

What started with a giggle soon turned into all out hysteria and other patrons were beginning to stare at us. In a futile attempt to hide, I sank further down in the chair.

Unfortunately, Rita didn't give me the same haircut as the girl in the poster and I left the salon sporting another Dorothy-do. On the drive home I stuck my head out of the car window, ever hopeful the wind would create the feral look I so desired.

I hurried into the house and headed straight for the bathroom. Staring back at me from the mirror was Dorothy Hamill's identical twin. I rubbed my head furiously, tousling my hair in all directions, convinced that it would help me achieve the look I so desperately wanted. Horrified, I watched lamely as every hair fell back into place.

I found a pair of scissors in the drawer and was deliberating which to cut first, my hair or my wrists, when the doorbell rang. I wasn't expecting anyone so I played off like I wasn't home, knowing whoever it was would eventually give up and go away.

The scissors were poised and ready to cut when some unknown force (the Queen Fairy, perhaps?) took charge of my body and ushered it to the front door. Peering through the peephole, I saw Shane with a bundle of flowers in one hand and a bottle of wine in the other. I opened the door just enough to stick my head through.

"Hi, Dusty," she said, reaching out to hand me the bouquet. "I hope this isn't a bad time. I just wanted to stop by and tell you how sorry I am for the horrible way I treated you the other night at the bar."

I opened the door slightly wider, took the flowers and replied flatly, "Thanks."

"So, this is where you live, huh? Nice house."

"Thanks."

She then handed me the bottle. I collected it from her and repeated, "Thanks."

"Maybe this was a bad idea. I should go."

"No."

"Okay… Can I come in? Or are you more at ease talking out here?"

"No," I stated again, fully aware that my vocabulary now consisted entirely of the two words, "thanks" and "no."

"I probably shouldn't have come," she muttered. "I'm sorry I bothered you."

"Forgive my rudeness, Shane. I'm just surprised to see you. Please, come in."

She followed me to the living room where I offered her a seat on the couch. A pack of cigarettes were lying on the table and she asked if she could have one. I tapped out two and kept one for myself. I lit hers first then watched as she inhaled deeply, the tip of the cigarette glowing as the smoke made its way into her body. A line of smoke trailed from her mouth as she paused to exhale.

"I had to see you," she said. "I couldn't leave things the way they were."

"How did you know where I live?"

"I'm embarrassed to admit that I followed you home from the bar that night. I sat in front of your house for half an hour. I wanted to talk to you then but figured you were still angry and needed more time to cool off. I've driven by several times since but didn't have the guts to stop. I am truly sorry, Dusty. Can you ever forgive me?"

Looking into her soft blue eyes, I felt my hardened heart begin to crumble.

"I'm at a loss here, Shane. I really don't know what to say."

Laying her hand over mine, she lowered her voice and continued.

"I'll do the talking then. You were right when you said I didn't know you very well. I would like to change that, if you'll give me the chance."

"Why should I give you that chance?"

"Because I promise to never hurt you like that again. I got a little crazy seeing that girl put her hands on you. It was a lot to process and I blew it."

Her unwavering stare and straightforward answers convinced me she was being sincere. I scanned her face for signs to the contrary but found none.

Curious to know her next move, I asked, "So, what is your plan?"

"I would very much like to get to know you better. And for you to know more about me as well."

Her eyes were pleading with me to ignore the red flags streaming inside my head, but I knew I had to think things through before answering. I tapped my cigarette against the rim of the ashtray and eased back onto the sofa. I held off an answer, postponing my response until I knew exactly what I wanted to say. Shane remained stoic the entire time with her eyes fixed on mine; unflinching, barely blinking.

"Okay," I said finally. "Maybe we could meet for dinner or something."

"Wonderful! There's a new Mediterranean restaurant that just opened around the corner from my store. We could meet there."

"All right."

"Let's say, Friday at six?"

I nodded to confirm. We exchanged smiles and then she mashed out her cigarette and rose from the couch.

"I better go before you realize what you've agreed to and change your mind," she said half-jokingly.

As I followed her to the door, the reality of what had just transpired started to soak in and I was a little unnerved by it. I felt an urge to say something else, but then she smiled at me and my mind went totally blank.

"I'm really excited about this," she offered, and then, looking me square in the eye, added, "There is one more thing…"

I held my breath, waiting for the proverbial bomb to drop. Instead, she reached out and ran her fingers through my hair.

"That haircut is adorable!" she said with a wink.

I stayed on the stoop until I could no longer see her car then hurried right back to the bathroom. After returning the scissors to the drawer, I glanced up at the mirror. The Queen Fairy and Angel were there, smiling and nodding their approval.

"Well done, Grasshopper," the Queen Fairy said. His palms were pressed together as if in prayer. "The stone, which represents courage, has been lifted from my hands. It now belongs to you. Use it wisely, my young friend."

"Isn't that line from Kung Fu?" the Angel smirked. "Seriously, Lewis. Couldn't you come up with something a bit more contemporary? That show hasn't been on in like a hundred years."

Turning to me, the Angel cleared her throat before speaking again. "Dusty…"

I was shocked. It was the first time she had ever addressed me directly.

"This is an unexpected surprise," I told her. "I've heard you talk to Lewis, but never to me."

She rolled her eyes in Lewis' direction and said, "I'm sure you see that I don't get many chances to speak when he's around."

"Yeah, I get that."

"Hello!" Lewis shouted. "I am right here!"

The Angel offered me a smile before continuing.

"You're a good person, Dusty. Don't lose sight of that and everything you want in this life will come to pass."

"Thank you, Angel. You too, Queenie. I appreciate all that you have done for me."

"Our job here is through," Lewis sighed, dabbing the pink feather boa against his cheek as though it were a tissue. "It's time to find someone else who needs our help, Angel Woman. Take care, Dusty. Remember to stay strong!"

"I will. Thank you both. For everything."

———————————————————————

I couldn't wait to tell my friends about Shane's visit, even though I already knew what their responses would be. The calling order was based solely on the support – or lack thereof – I expected to get in return. First would be Marge (anti-Shane), then Butch (pro-Shane), and last but not least, Biff (the voice of reason).

Marge, the toughest nut in our group, was flabbergasted. Suffice it to say she was nowhere near as ecstatic about the possibility of my reconnecting with Shane as I was.

"Are you fucking nuts? That woman ripped you to shreds at the bar and you are letting her back in your life? Have you no shame? Have you no pride?"

"She asked for another chance, Marge. I think I should give it to her."

"And I think you should have your head examined."

"So, you're against it?"

"I think you're moving way too fast. You need to give it more time."

"It's just a first date, Marge. We're not running off to get married."

"Do what you want, Dusty. It's your decision."

One down, two to go.

Butch was the softie of the bunch and I could pretty much tell her anything and she would agree with it. And I was right. She did.

"I'm very happy for you, Dusty. If you really like her, I say go for it."

Okay, no surprises so far. Butch is in favor of the reconciliation and Marge is against it. Now it was up to Biff to cast her vote and break the tie.

Biff was the most grounded, levelheaded person I had ever met. Her opinion meant the world to me and I knew I should give her answer serious consideration. If she said yes, I would definitely follow through with the date. If she said no, I would be inclined to cancel.

"What do you want to happen, Dusty?"

"I think she deserves another chance, Biff. If I had screwed things up that badly I would want another chance. Wouldn't you?"

"I'm 99% sure I would have never been in a predicament like this in the first place. I rarely act on hasty decisions. In the second place, I highly doubt…"

"Yeah, yeah. Let's not overanalyze this. 'Yes' or 'No.' It's that simple."

"Nothing is ever that simple, Dusty."

"Then go with your gut on this one, Biff. Whaddya say?"

"All right then. I think you should…"

—— THAT'S AMORE ——

It was a few minutes before six when I arrived at the restaurant. Shane was waiting at the door and hugged me when I approached.

"Table for two?" the greeter inquired.

"Yes," she replied. "It's just the two of us."

After escorting us to our seats, he was quickly replaced by a waiter asking to take our drink orders.

"I'd like a glass of white wine," I told him. "Preferably, Chardonnay."

"Chardonnay for me as well," Shane echoed.

We both then fell silent, each one waiting for the other to speak. Shane was the first to take the lead.

"Thanks for agreeing to this," she said. "Wow. There are so many things I want to say to you that I don't really know where to begin."

I sat quietly while she put her words in order. Moments later, she started again.

"Ever since we met, my thoughts and emotions have been scattered and that is so out of character for me. Most people know me as being calm and sensible, but I'm feeling things now that I have never felt before and it has me a little out of sorts. My hope is that in getting to know one another, I'll find clarity in all of this.

"I'm drawn to you in ways I can't explain or even fully comprehend. When I found out that you were a lesbian, I started thinking that if I liked you and you were gay, did that make me gay, too? Then, after what happened at your office Christmas party, I began to question everything about myself."

The conversation was put on hold as the waiter returned with our drinks. Placing them on the table, he asked, "Are you ready to order?"

"Not yet," I told him. "Can you give us a few more minutes?"

He nodded, and Shane began again as soon as he left.

"That time when we, well, you know… Not a day goes by that I don't think about it. My feelings for you are intriguing and enticing, but they also scare the hell out of me."

"Oh," I responded. That was it. That was all I could muster.

It seemed like she wanted to say something else but then stopped herself. I waited for her to go on but she didn't offer anything else, leaving me to wonder what would come next. Was she still interested in satisfying her curiosity? Or had she realized she'd taken a wrong turn somewhere?

As if to grant her an even longer reprieve, the pause was extended when the waiter returned to collect our dinner choices. Wearing a smile that looked like it had been pasted onto his face, he asked, "Would you like to order now?"

I wanted to dismiss him again to give Shane more time to continue. Before I had a chance to speak, she picked up her menu and, without looking at it, handed it back to him.

"I'll have the special," she said.

"But I haven't told you what that is," he objected.

"I'm feeling a little risqué tonight," she said teasingly. "How about you, Dusty?"

"I'm game."

She then told the waiter, "Two specials, please."

The young man walked away but stopped after a few steps and turned back to look at us, grinning and shaking his head. By the time he reached the kitchen he was laughing out loud. Neither of us said much after our food arrived, so we finished our meals and left the restaurant.

"That went well, don't you think?" Shane asked once we were outside.

I wasn't sure how to respond, so I just nodded. I had no idea how her story would end until she at last confided, "I think what I've been trying to tell you is that I'm not sure what this thing is between us, but I owe it to myself, and to you, to figure it out."

She came forward, wrapped her arms around my neck and kissed me on the cheek. After separating, she announced, "Next time, let's have dinner at my place. That bottle of wine I gave you pairs well with spaghetti. You do like spaghetti, don't you?"

"I love spaghetti."

"I've been told I make a scrumptious sauce. I hope you'll agree."

"I'm sure I will."

"Are you free on Tuesday?"

"Yes. Yes, I am."

"Perfect! I'll see you on Tuesday!"

-- -- -- -- -- -- -- -- -- -- -- -- -- -- -- --

Shane lived in a two-story condominium decorated with an assortment of tokens from faraway places, a menagerie of artifacts that captivated your attention the moment you walked in the door. A small entryway led into the living room where logs crackling in the fireplace cast a dim halo of light around the mantel. In the adjoining room I could see a hand-carved mahogany table littered with an assortment of brightly burning candles of various colors and sizes. A thick, crystal vase filled with fresh-cut flowers sat in the middle of the table, standing watch over all of the flames.

Shane met me at the door dressed in a multi-colored sweater and white slacks; her flaxen hair twisted into a loose bun. She ushered me inside and planted a kiss on my lips before returning to the kitchen to tend to her sauce.

"Feel free to wander around while I finish up in here," she said.

"Do you need any help?"

"Nope. I'm good."

"Ain't that the truth," I mumbled.

"Did you say something?"

"Nothing I'm brave enough to repeat."

"Okay. Go ahead and make yourself at home. Mi casa es su casa."

I set the wine on the table then ventured down the hallway, stopping outside a pair of French doors that opened to her bedroom. White sateen material draped the canopied edges of a colonial style bed, the corner pieces cinched together by a braided, silk cord. The comforter had been folded back to reveal satin sheets underneath.

My mind was lost in a fantasy of the two of us together in that bed when she called me to dinner. I had no idea how long I'd been standing in that doorway, but enough time had passed that I never made it to any of the other rooms.

After dinner we snuggled on the couch, the Carpenter's crooning in the background as we conversed and sipped wine from oversized goblets. Shane shared more stories about her life, offering candid details about her family.

She came from old money, she told me, an offspring from a long line of American politicians. Her two times great-grandfather, Jameson Tucker DuBois, served as German Consul, then transferred to the same role in Switzerland and Singapore before ending his career as U.S. Minister to Persia in the early 1900s. Her great-grandfather, Mason, served as Secretary to the U.S. Minister, who, at the time, was his father. An avid traveler, Mason made frequent trips across Europe, Asia, Africa and South America, and, by the end of his travels had amassed an impressive collection of native artifacts. Those trinkets, combined with the ones collected by his father, were passed to his son, Shane's grandfather, Jackson.

Jackson DuBois was a famous fighter pilot who flew combat missions in the South Pacific during World War II. After the war he joined a handful of other pilots to start an airline carrier service in the region, which eventually became the predecessor to Pan Am Airlines. Jackson, Jr., Shane's father, had a love for flying that matched her grandfather's and swore his allegiance to the Air Force when he was eighteen. Prior to enlisting, he wed his high school sweetheart, Francis, and they were relocated to the United Kingdom after his graduation from induction training. Shane came into their lives a year and a half later. Their time in England was short-lived as the first of many reassignment orders followed to transfer the family to Germany (where her brother, Michael, was born), Azores, Turkey and Italy, and then across the ocean to Virginia. His final orders landed them at Carswell Air Force Base in Fort Worth. A year later, he retired and moved his family to Houston.

As a young child, Shane took a keen interest in the collectibles that had been passed to her father and would add trinkets of her own at every base they were stationed. While they were in Turkey she visited her first bazaar, which she described to me as an enclosed marketplace that sold goods in exchange for services. Only fourteen at the time, she knew that her life's calling would be in the trade industry as well.

At twenty-five, she packed her diplomas from Sam Houston University alongside her artifacts and a few personal belongings and moved to Dallas to start a business of her own. Michael followed three years later. Frances came along after her father passed away from a heart attack in 1994.

"And that's how I ended up here," she stated matter-of-factly.

Now that her tale was over, Shane asked me to share details of my own life. I opted to skip my childhood altogether and start my story at the time I joined the military. As I described the investigation that ended my career, she lifted the bottle and topped off our glasses.

"Have you ever been in love?" she asked when I had finished.

"What brought that up?"

"You mentioned a couple of women, but you talk as though they were nothing more than casual acquaintances. Has there ever been anyone special? You know, someone you were madly in love with?"

"Once, maybe. What about you?"

"I was engaged twice. As you can tell, neither one made it to the altar."

"Why not?"

"I couldn't see either relationship going the distance. I loved them both very much but I wasn't *in* love. I knew it would only be a matter of time before the lights went out."

"So, you were the one that called it quits? Both times?"

"Yes. I was too busy to be tied down. I know that sounds selfish, but it's the truth. I enjoyed my freedom and all the privileges that came with it. They both expected me to give up my business – turn it over to Michael – and start making plans for a family. Well, that's not the order I had in mind for my life. I've worked hard for my success and wasn't willing to give it up. Not then. Not now. Not ever."

"I can't blame you. I wouldn't want to give all of that up either."

"Enough about me. I want to hear more about your one true love."

I took a deep breath and let it out slowly. Talking about my past would only open old wounds and I didn't want to go there. Not now. Not while things were going so well. As thoughts of Alison crept into my mind, I became fidgety, repositioning my body several times before finally settling back into the cushions on the sofa.

"Is something wrong?" she asked.

"No."

"Do you not want to talk about her?"

"There's nothing to tell."

"Sure, there is. Why else would you be acting so nervous?"

"I'm not nervous. I'm just uncomfortable talking about it."

"Why? Did something bad happen?"

"Not really."

"If it wasn't bad, then why won't you tell me?"

"All right. She said she loved me and it freaked me out."

"Why did that freak you out?"

"Because it was foreign to me."

"Having someone say they love you?"

"Yeah. Pretty weird, huh?"

"Didn't your parents tell you they loved you?"

"I don't ever remember my dad saying it to me. My mom only said it when she sent me away for the summers. Right before she put me on a plane."

"Why did she send you away?"

"I guess she didn't want me around."

"How old were you?"

"The first time? Around four or five, I think."

"My God. That is horrible."

What was more horrific was that the past I wanted to stay buried had resurfaced and I was telling Shane things that weren't meant to be shared with anyone. Ever.

"What about your dad?"

"He was actually my stepfather. We were really close when I was young but that all changed as I got older. He was pretty quiet; never really said much of anything."

"And your real father?"

"Never knew him."

Drawing me into her arms, she whispered, "You poor thing."

"Don't pity me," I replied harshly while pulling away from her.

"I'm not. I just can't imagine having to go through childhood like that."

"I survived."

"Yeah, but at what cost? What did you lose in the process? Love?"

I took another sip of wine and stared into my lap, humbled and mortified at having exposed myself like that. Silence clung to the air like dew on the morning grass and the stillness was making me uneasy. I finally broke through the quiet by saying, "I should go. Thanks for dinner, Shane."

"Don't leave," she pleaded.

I swiped at a stray tear rolling down my cheek with the back of my wrist, more than a little pissed that I was on the verge of bawling. Shane reached behind me to grab a box of tissues and continued, her words hypnotically soothing my fractured ego.

"I can tell you've had a lot of pain in your life, Dusty. I can't take that away but I'd like to show you what happiness is supposed to feel like."

Caressing the side of my face, she purred, "Please. Don't go."

I ripped a tissue from the box and blotted the cascade of tears now streaming down my face then grabbed another and draped it over my eyes to hide my shame. Shane pulled it away and prodded again, "Stay, Dusty. Please?"

The answer I blurted out was short and succinct, void of emotion. "Fine."

She left the couch and went to the kitchen to retrieve another bottle of wine. When she returned, she refilled our glasses then scooted closer to me and laid her head on my shoulder. We stayed like that until she fell asleep in my arms. I continued to stare at the fire, a million thoughts racing through my mind until the last log burned itself out. As the hours passed, one thought remained constant: Shane was the key that could unlock the door to my happiness.

- -

My eyes were opened the next morning by the smell of something delicious filling my nostrils. Sunlight was peering through the blinds while birds warbled chirpy tunes just outside the window. I was alone on the couch; Shane was nowhere in sight. At some point during the night, she had covered me with a small blanket, which I held under my chin as I scanned the room for her.

My joyous awakening then took a dramatic turn, replaced by an unexpected wave of melancholy. A lump formed in my throat at the same time tears started pooling in my eyes. I had no idea why I was in such a state – again – and, before I could collect myself, Shane entered the room with a tray of food and set it on the coffee table.

"What's wrong?" she asked, bending forward to plant a kiss on my forehead.

Sobbing, I answered, "I don't know."

"Did you have a nightmare?"

"No. It just came over me a little while ago."

She paused briefly, eyeing me inquisitively.

"Maybe it has something to do with our discussion last night."

"What do you mean?"

"I think you might be afraid of what I represent."

"What is it that you represent?"

"Love, silly."

"You think I'm afraid of love?"

"I do. More so than I was in the beginning, but look at me now!"

With a wink and a smile, she smeared a dollop of jelly onto the tip of my nose. She was already proving herself successful at blazing a trail into my heart and bringing down walls faster than I could resurrect them.

"Are we moving too fast?" she asked after removing the jelly with a napkin. "Is that what is scaring you?"

"I think my past is what scares me. I've been alone for a long time. It's what I know. It's who I am."

"What can I do to help you?"

"Don't give up on me. Give me time to work through this."

She lowered herself onto the cushion and brought her face close to mine.

"I will never give up on you, Dusty," she vowed. "That's a promise."

She kept that promise, generously taking precautions to keep me far from the pains of my past, and, day by day, my feelings grew stronger. One night, we went to see *Phantom of the Opera* at the old, Majestic Theater. Throughout the performance I felt drawn to the phantom on a deeply personal level. All he wanted was for someone to love him, someone to call his own. When he sang *The Music of the Night*, I was genuinely moved to tears. The lyrics "close your eyes and surrender to your darkest dream" rang true, as if Andrew Webber had penned them especially for me.

The entire performance affected me in ways I could never have imagined and I was having a hard time reeling in my emotions. Shane saw me crying and slid her arm through mine to offer comfort. She had seen the show many times and knew the words to all of the songs by heart. Pulling me close, she sang along in a low, whispery voice, "Open up your mind; let your fantasies unwind." And then she kissed me. Square on the lips, right there on the front row of that historic theater.

She continued holding my arm as we left the building and walked to her car.

"What did you think of the opera?" she asked once we were inside.

"Oh my God," I muttered. "I have no words to describe it."

"Try."

"I feel exposed in a way. Kinda raw. Does that make sense?"

"It does. This was a big night for you, wasn't it?"

"Yes. I'm feeling things I've never felt before – things I was never *allowed* to feel before."

"I'm glad I was here to experience this with you."

"So am I. Very much so."

—— AT LONG LAST, LOVE ——

Many things were discussed that first night at Shane's condo, but what didn't come up, intentional or not, was any further mention of what happened at the office party, nor did either of us make an attempt to initiate anything new. It was about connecting on an emotional and spiritual level, not a physical one.

I assumed and was comfortable with the idea that Shane and I would not be having sexual relations again until we had an opportunity to get to know one another better. Two weeks after she appeared on my front stoop with the bouquet of flowers and bottle of wine it happened, way sooner than I had anticipated.

It was eight o'clock in the morning and I was barely out of bed when the doorbell rang. Still in my nightclothes, an oversized football jersey and the baggiest pair of boxers I could find in my underwear drawer, I opened the door and saw Shane standing on my porch with a huge grin on her face.

"Are you ready?" she asked.

"Ready for what?"

I hadn't even had my first cup of coffee or my first cigarette, and my teeth weren't brushed. Neither was my hair, which had formed into clumps overnight with each clump sticking out in a different direction.

Shane, on the other hand, was neatly dressed in a snug pair of jeans and a T-shirt with a sweater tied loosely around her shoulders. There was a slight chill in the air and it was obvious she wasn't wearing a bra. Coffee was my usual morning stimulant, but seeing her nipples was providing a much more pleasurable alternative to caffeine.

"Were you still in bed?" she asked.

"No," I responded, my voice still crackling with the sound of sleep. I motioned for her to come inside. "I've been up for a bit. I just made a pot of coffee. Want some?"

After crossing the threshold, she turned to me and smiled. The light in the hallway shone in her eyes, illuminating the same shade of blue that colored the morning sky just outside my door.

"Cups are beside the coffee maker," I told her. "Help yourself while I get a shower."

She nodded before heading toward the kitchen. She must have sensed I was staring as she walked down the hall because she stopped briefly and called back over her shoulder, "See something that you like?"

"Yeah. The view is spectacular from back here."

"Maybe later you can have a closer look. Go get cleaned up now. I'll be waiting."

Racing to the bathroom, I tore off my clothes and tossed them onto the floor then ran a dry toothbrush across my teeth and grabbed a towel from a stack of linens under the sink. My heart was pounding with excitement as I turned on the water to let it heat up. As soon as I stepped into the shower, there was a knock on the bathroom door.

I wrapped the curtain around my torso and peered out from behind it.

"Yes?" I called out. "Can I help you?"

Shane opened the door far enough to poke her head in.

"Where do you keep the sugar?" she asked.

"In the pantry. Blue Tupperware container."

Instead of returning to the kitchen for the sugar, she pushed the door open the rest of the way and came toward me. The hot water, coupled with the heat from my over-active hormones, had birthed countless beads of perspiration over the entire surface of my body.

She moved in front of me and kissed the tip of my nose then lowered her head to nuzzle my neck. I started blowing puffs of air on my upper lip to cool off, which seemed to have no more effect than using a garden hose on a raging wildfire.

"I thought you wanted sugar," I said facetiously.

Positioning her mouth next to my ear, she whispered, "I do."

She leaned away from me to reach into the shower and turn off the water then drew back the curtain. Steam immediately engulfed the room, wetting her shirt and causing the fabric to cling to her chest, outlining the full shape of her breasts.

"It sure is hot in here," she said.

"It sure is," I echoed.

"Wanna go somewhere even hotter?"

I barely managed to wrap the towel around my midsection before she dragged me to the bedroom. Standing beside the bedpost, she pulled the towel away and it fell to the floor, landing in a heap around my ankles.

She struggled with trying to remove her damp shirt while I was making incredible strides unzipping her jeans and guiding them over her hips. She wasn't wearing anything underneath, which created a whole new rash of moisture on my already soaked body.

I helped her out of her shirt then eased her onto the bed and started a trail of kisses from her neck to her navel, then let my mouth navigate through her pubic hair and across the folds of skin surrounding her clitoris. The full, round organ pressed firmly against my tongue as her hips began to slowly move back and forth. When their tempo accelerated, I slid two fingers inside of her and a warm rush of fluids seeped out onto my palm.

Her thigh muscles quivered while my fingers pumped in and out, faster and harder with each thrust. She held my head with both hands to anchor my mouth in place, arching her back and raising her hips while spasms shook her body in the final moments before climax. A satisfied grin filled her face when she let out a long, heavy sigh afterwards.

"That was amazing," she said, now smiling broadly. "I don't think I can top that."

"It isn't a competition, Shane. You don't have to..."

She quickly cut me off and purred, "Oh, but I want to."

Rolling me onto my stomach she laid on top of me, her hips continuing to gyrate as though I were still inside of her. I could feel her nipples hardening as she pressed them against my ribcage. She then moved alongside of me and began gliding her fingers back and forth across the lower part of my back. It wasn't long before she discovered the base of my spine was overly sensitive and set up camp there, her tender caress generating chills and waves of goosebumps with every stroke. Each touch caused me to jerk and gasp in response. My reactions were giving her great pleasure and she showed no signs of letting up. I finally had to grab her hand to end the pleasurable torture.

"What are you doing?" she asked with a tone of indignance.

"Stopping you," I moaned in response.

"Why? I was enjoying myself."

"I know, but you were killing me in the process."

I maneuvered out from under her and rolled onto my back then adjusted myself to where her head was above my crotch. She rested her chin on my pubic bone (not what I was aiming for) and exhaled loudly through her nose, a clear indication she was not happy with the new arrangement.

"I wish you hadn't stopped me," she pouted. "The way your body was moving and the noises you were making... It was a real turn on."

"Yeah? Well, I've been turned on since you rang the doorbell."

"Really?"

"See for yourself."

She scooted her body up until her hips were wedged between my thighs then raised them high enough to squeeze her hand in underneath. Her mouth sealed over my breast at the same time her fingers came in contact with my vagina.

"Oh my," she exclaimed through a mouthful of nipple. "You are incredibly wet."

In truth, I was dripping. But she already knew that.

Her breathing became labored, her ribcage heaving as she pushed her way deeper inside of me. We made love again and again, a feat I had never accomplished with anyone before her. I have no idea how many orgasms I had that morning. I lost count after five.

We held each other afterwards and I listened as the pace of her breathing changed from fast to slow to the relaxed cadence of slumber. Only after she was asleep did I close my eyes. Three hours would pass before they opened again.

I awoke fully energized, which was astonishing since I still hadn't had my first cup of coffee. My stomach was grumbling, a reminder that I had also skipped breakfast. Not wanting to wake Shane, I quietly left the bed and draped a small blanket over her.

At the door I turned for another look at her – the erotic woman that had so quickly turned my uneventful life into one filled with passion and intrigue. This was so much more than an infatuation. I was smitten.

I wanted to linger in that space forever but my withdrawals were kicking in and I knew the only way to satisfy them was with a jolt of java. I grabbed my jersey on the way out and yanked it over my head in route to the kitchen. After starting a fresh pot of coffee, I sat at the table with an empty mug in one hand and a cigarette in the other while waiting for the percolator to finish. I inhaled the first cup then poured a second and carried it with me back to the bedroom.

A flood of unfamiliar feelings washed over me as I leaned against the doorjamb.

Is this what love feels like? I wondered.

Shane's eyes opened and her tiny breasts poked out from under the blanket as she stretched her arms high above her head.

"What time is it?" she asked, yawning.

"Noonish."

"Is there any more coffee?"

"Yes. Stay there and I'll get you a cup. How much sugar do you take?"

"I drink it black."

"Black? Wait a minute. I distinctly remember…"

"I needed an excuse to come into the bathroom. Asking for sugar was the first thing that came to mind."

I smiled and took a sip of my drink, completely blanking out the offer I had made to get her a cup as well. Within seconds, she voiced a subtle reminder.

"Dusty?"

"Yes?"

"The coffee?"

"Oh shit. My mind was totally somewhere else. I'll be right back."

Halfway to the kitchen, I heard her footsteps in the hallway behind me.

"Ummm," she hummed melodically. "That coffee sure smells good. It's making me kind of hungry, too."

"There isn't much here. On weekends, I normally eat at the diner."

Shane stuck her head inside the refrigerator. The blanket was pulled up around her shoulders, her bare butt sticking out from underneath.

"Mind if I look around? I'm sure there's something in here I can nibble on."

"Okay. Good luck with that."

After scouring empty shelves, she let go of the door and shook her head.

"Wow, you weren't kidding. There isn't *anything* in there."

"I told you. I'll treat you to lunch after I take a quick shower. Be back in a flash."

"I'll have starved to death by then. Do you have any crackers?"

"Check the pantry."

Her feet slapped loudly against the linoleum as she moved to the other side of the room. She found a half-full box of Saltines on the top shelf and carried them to the table.

"These are stale," she said as she sat down across from me. Crumbs were spewing from her mouth as she spoke.

"There's no telling how long that box has been in there," I admitted with a tinge of embarrassment.

"There has to be something to eat around here. Do you mind if I keep looking?"

"Help yourself."

Every drawer and cabinet was thoroughly explored, but the results were the same as Shane continued to come up empty-handed. Flopping down into her chair, she groaned and shoved another fistful of crackers into her mouth.

"I will leave you with those while I take my shower," I said, grinning.

Less than fifteen minutes later, I returned to find that she had finished off not only the entire box of Saltines, but the rest of the coffee as well.

"Ready for lunch?" I inquired.

She let out a slight belch and giggled, her cheeks blushed in crimson as she placed her hand over her mouth.

"Sorry. That was rude of me. Guess I ate too many crackers."

When she leaned forward to claim her empty coffee cup, the blanket slid from her shoulders to down around her waist. Being the self-conscious type, I would have instantly pulled it back up. Shane, however, made no attempt to do so.

She has absolutely no inhibitions, I concluded. *I love that about her.*

She looked at me and smiled and I had to peel my eyes away from her breasts to do the same in return. A split second later, my gaze went right back to her chest.

That's the second time I used the word "love" today, I acknowledged silently.

Instead of going out, we ended up ordering pizza and spent the rest of the afternoon nibbling on it – and each other – between the sheets.

While I was gathering up the trash to throw away, Shane confessed her reasons for coming over that morning.

"I hope you don't mind my just showing up like I did."

"Not at all," I reassured her.

"I have wanted to do that since that night you stayed at my condo." She gave me a quick wink and added, "I'm putting that out there first to get it out of the way."

She paused then, her eyebrows raised as she formulated her next statement.

"That's not the only reason I'm here. The bigger reason is this... There's something I need to tell you."

I didn't know where she was going with her comment so I sat quietly and waited.

"I'm sure you're not ready to hear this," she continued, "and it's probably not the best time to say it, but I really care about you and I'm fairly certain you feel the same way about me. I'm falling in love with you, Dusty. I think it started that first day at your store when I asked you to help me with the boxes."

"Really? I thought you were only looking for cheap labor."

"Be serious."

"Sorry."

"And then at the Christmas party – you were so tender and so passionate. It truly captured my heart."

"I had no idea you felt that way."

"I didn't want to say anything before now because I thought it might scare you off."

"You're right. It probably would have."

As I looked in her eyes, that same sensation I experienced earlier that morning in the bedroom doorway filled me once again.

"So, now that I have spilled my guts," Shane said, "how do you feel about me?"

I lowered my head to intentionally avoid her gaze.

"Don't be afraid," she offered reassuringly. "I'll accept whatever you tell me."

With my chin still hanging just above my chest, I let these words pass slowly across my lips: "I'm falling in love with you, too, Shane."

While my tone was barely audible, she reacted as though I had shouted it from the rooftop. Looping her arms around my neck, she squealed, "See how easy that was?"

I'm sure the expression on my face showed her how excruciating it was for me to make that kind of proclamation. I suddenly felt vulnerable and exposed and wanted to recant, to take it all back and pretend it never happened.

"You look like you're about to be executed," she said jokingly.

She couldn't have been more right. That was exactly how I felt.

- -

After a couple months of dating, Shane let her brother, Michael, and his girlfriend take over the lease on her condo and moved into my place. Biff and Butch were elated that she had become a permanent part of my life and invited us to The Corral, a gay western bar, to celebrate the occasion. Marge, still on the fence about the entire Shane/Dusty affair was coming, too, but only for the "drinking and dancing" she told Biff, and not to celebrate something she felt would more than likely be short-lived.

Shane had never been to a western bar and wanted to buy a pair of boots and a hat to better look the part. Now that we were living together, I discovered how much she loved to shop (evidenced by the number of times I was beckoned to the mall) and how often she would jump on any opportunity to expand her wardrobe. On the eve of our big outing, she pranced into the living room wearing nothing more than her two latest purchases.

"Well?" she asked, her hands planted firmly on her hips as she sashayed up to the couch. "What do you think?"

"About the boots or the hat?"

"Either. Or both."

"I like the naked part in between the best."

The soft brim of her hat tapped against my forehead as she bent down to kiss me. Climbing onto my lap, she purred, "So you like my outfit, huh?"

"If that's all you're wearing tomorrow night," I grinned, pulling her close, "you will have a very full dance card, that's for sure. And you'll probably end up with more friends than you can shake a stick at when the dancing is done."

"What about you, Dusty? Will you be my friend?"

"I'll be whatever you want me to be, Shane."

"Glad to hear that because there's something I want to ask you."

"Uh-oh. I'm not liking the sound of this."

Her breasts were now pressed against mine with only the thin material of my shirt between them. Our nipples hardened simultaneously upon contact.

"I have a fantasy," she said softly, as if there were others around to overhear.

"Cool! Is it kinky?"

"Dusty," she bellowed, sitting upright. Her face was blood red. "It's hard enough to say this as it is. Don't make it any harder."

"I'm sorry. What is your fantasy?"

"Have you ever been tied up?"

I smiled and tweaked her nipple.

"Is that part of the fantasy?"

"Maybe," she answered, smacking my hand. "Just answer the question."

"No, I haven't. There was never a reason to. I gave my body freely to anyone who asked. Why? Are you planning to tie me up?"

Putting her hands on my shoulders, she stared directly into my eyes.

"I might, if you don't cooperate."

While the thought of bondage did pique my interest, I wasn't sure how long the excitement would last with my extremities purposely held in check. I decided it probably wouldn't be such a good idea in the long run.

"Come with me," she said in a commanding tone.

"Where?"

"To the bedroom."

"Now?"

The look I got in return assured me that I had better get up and get moving. Once there, she ordered me to take off my clothes and close my eyes then continued to dole out instructions that I wasn't to open them again until given permission to do so.

"There's no talking either," she added as an afterthought. "Not a peep. Got it?"

Eyes closed tightly, I dipped my chin to affirm that I understood the demands being placed upon me. After helping me onto the mattress, I heard her leave the room. Tempting as it was, I didn't open my eyes, knowing my punishment would most likely involve some kind of tethering – ropes, or, worse yet, handcuffs.

So, there I was, naked as a jaybird on the bed all by my lonesome. The modest half of my personality wanted to cover up with *something* while the tits-to-the-wind half was content lying in wait to see what would happen next. My emotions were still at war when she returned. Plopping down beside me, she extended my arms upward and tucked my hands behind my head.

"Your eyes are still closed, right?"

I nodded, not sure if I had yet been authorized to speak.

There was a slight popping noise followed by the smell of chocolate. A line of cold liquid was drawn from my chin to my abdomen, then from one nipple to the other. Shane lowered her body onto mine and started sliding from side to side to smear the concoction onto her own chest, then sat upright and squirted a generous amount into my belly button and seated herself atop the newly made puddle. I heard a cap snapping shut just before she tossed whatever she was holding onto the floor.

Her warm breath filled my ear as she whispered for me to open my eyes. There, poised before my face, was a chocolate covered nipple. The gag order completely forgotten by this point, I opened my mouth to speak. She quickly laid a finger over my lips and said, "No talking, remember? You say one word and I'm going to tie you up."

She glared at me long after removing her finger, fully intent on making damn sure I knew who was in charge of this expedition down Fantasy Lane. Stared into submission but still brave enough to call her bluff, I mouthed the word 'Okay' and smiled.

She ordered me to lick the chocolate off of her breast. Its twin was presented next, and I was told to clean it as well. When both were spotless, she inched her way toward the headboard, her pubic hair brushing against my chin as she straddled my face. Her hips began moving in slow, grinding circles and I was soon coated with a sticky combination of her body fluids and syrup. She gripped the bedpost while I lapped at her clit, orgasmic spurts of cum mixed with chocolate trickling down my throat as she climaxed. She wanted a kiss afterwards, but the chocolate had dried to a hard crust and I was unable to open my mouth far enough to accommodate.

Still playing along that I wasn't allowed to speak (and unsure I could part my lips even if I wanted to), I mimed the motions of taking a shower. Shane wanted to stay behind and rest but pledged to join me a few minutes later. I stood under the water until it started to run cold but she never made it. Naturally, I assumed she had fallen asleep.

As I was drying off, I heard a muffled whimper followed by a thump. I immediately became concerned and called out, "Shane?"

I waited, but no answer came. When I yanked the door open, I saw her lying on the floor next to the bed. Hurrying to her side, I dropped to my knees and, in a panic, tried to find a pulse. Not getting the response I wanted, I placed my ear over her breastbone and gave a sigh of relief after hearing a strong heartbeat.

"Shane," I said again, shaking her lightly. "Can you hear me?"

There was still no response, so I grabbed the phone off of the nightstand and dialed 911, then slipped on a pair of sweats and sat beside her until the ambulance arrived. After the initial assessment, one of the paramedics asked if the brown substance on her body might possibly have any toxic properties.

I cocked my head to the side and scowled at him before offering a reply.

"Toxic properties?" I echoed. "It's chocolate syrup, for Christ's sake!"

I picked up the bottle and placed it in his hands. He lifted the cap, waved it under his nose and inhaled deeply, then nodded an affirmation to his partner.

The other paramedic turned to me and said, "It could be an allergic reaction. We should take the bottle with us to the hospital in case they need to run some tests."

"Whatever. Please, just hurry!"

While they were strapping Shane to the gurney, I called Butch and told her what had happened (purposely leaving out the part about the syrup) and asked if she would meet me at the hospital. She agreed to come as soon as possible. Before hanging up with her, I asked if she would call Marge and Biff to let them know as well.

I scooped up Shane's clothes and handed them to one of the technicians as they were transporting her out the front door and onto the sidewalk. I followed closely behind until they lifted her into the ambulance. One of the men jumped in with her at the same time the other reached for the doors to close them inside.

"Wait," I said, grabbing his arm. "I'm going with her."

"Only spouses and immediate family are allowed in there," he said. "You'll have to follow in your own car."

"But she is my girlfriend!"

"Sorry, lady. Rules are rules."

"Fuck your rules! Open those doors, damn it! I am getting in that ambulance!"

The technician with Shane pushed the doors open and motioned for me to enter.

"Come on," he said. "Get in."

His partner quickly started to voice his disapproval.

"But Roy…"

"Bill," he countered, cutting him off before he could further his complaint. "She's right. We should bend the rules on this one."

I held Shane's hand the entire ride to the hospital. She didn't regain consciousness before our arrival but her vitals were strong and Roy assured me that she was going to be okay. Before wheeling her into Triage, he directed me to a waiting area. I watched a team of nurses form a circle around the gurney while Roy relayed her statistics.

"What is that brown stuff?" one of them asked.

"Chocolate syrup," Bill answered. "We brought it with us," he added, displaying the bottle as if he were a showcase hostess on a television game show.

The nurse at Shane's head began to chuckle, and soon everyone gathered around her was laughing as well. The snickering continued as they steered the gurney through the double doors into one of the examination rooms.

■ ■ ■ ■ ■ ■ ■ ■ ■ ■ ■ ■ ■ ■ ■ ■ ■ ■ ■ ■

I challenged every person who came through those doors for an update on Shane. Nearly an hour would pass before any real news emerged: she was awake and responsive. The woman making the announcement had on a white medical coat with the name "Dr. Brisdale" embroidered in dark blue stitching just below the lapel.

"Can I see her?" I asked.

"Are you a family member?"

"Yes," I lied. "I'm her sister."

"Okay, but don't stay too long. She's in Bed 12. It's on the right."

The doctor waved her badge in front of a sensor pad labeled "Staff Only" and the doors opened automatically. I passed through quickly, peering behind every curtain until I found Shane.

She greeted me with a soft "Hi" as I entered the room.

"Hi yourself. How are you feeling?"

"Better. Still kind of groggy, but better."

"Looks like they cleaned you up."

"Yes, thank goodness. The nurse had a heck of a time washing that syrup off."

"Have they figured out what's wrong?"

"Not yet. The doctor is supposed to be here soon to go over the test results."

"Okay. I'll come back later so you can talk in private."

"Would you do me a favor on your way out?"

"Sure."

"Call my brother and tell him I'm here. Ask him to call Mom and let her know, too."

"No problem."

I grabbed a pen from the cart and jotted her brother's number on the palm of my hand. Before leaving, I kissed her on the forehead.

"Get some rest," I said. "I'll be back soon."

Back in the waiting room, I shoved my hands in my pockets to search for coins for the payphone. With everything that had happened, I completely forgot to bring money or identification. I shared my predicament with the receptionist, who was kind enough to let me use the hospital phone to call Shane's brother.

When Michael answered, I introduced myself and explained the reason for my call (once again leaving out the part about the syrup). He told me he would pick up his mother and come immediately to the hospital. I offered to wait for them in the lobby.

Before returning the phone, I asked the receptionist if I could make another call. After getting her approval, I dialed Butch's number and she picked up on the first ring.

"When are you coming?" I asked.

"I'm just now leaving work. I should be there in about thirty minutes."

"Take your time. Shane is still in the Emergency Room."

"You got to see her?"

"Yeah, but only for a minute."

"How's she doing? Better yet, how are you doing? Do you need anything?"

"My ID. And some money. I totally forgot both."

"I can swing by your house on the way over. Is the key still under the potted plant?"

"Yeah, same place as always. Thanks, Butch. See you in a bit."

Marge and Biff came charging through the lobby doors as I was handing the phone back to the receptionist.

"What happened?" Marge blurted out as they were approaching.

"I don't know yet. They ran some tests, but…"

Biff interrupted to ask, "How is she now?"

"She's still pretty weak but everyone seems to think she's going to be okay."

Marge draped her arm over my shoulders and gave me a motherly squeeze.

"How are you doing? You want anything?"

"Something to drink would be nice."

"Are you hungry?"

"Yeah, a little bit."

"Let's go to the cafeteria. It will probably be a while before you hear anything."

"I can't. I told her brother I would wait for him here. Besides, everything happened so fast that I forgot to bring any cash."

"No problem," Biff said, smiling. "I've got you covered."

She left and returned a short while later with a steaming cup of coffee and a bag of Peanut M&M's. Not long after, Butch arrived carrying a cold bottle of Dr. Pepper and a Butterfinger. If all the anxiety and worry hadn't been enough to keep me on my toes as it was, that much caffeine and (more) chocolate would surely do the trick.

A pair of chatty women were coming toward us as Butch was handing me my drink and one of them accidentally bumped into her. Turning to face her afterwards, the woman said, "Excuse me, sir."

"No problem," Butch answered.

As they continued on, I heard that woman say to her companion, "Oh my God! Did you know that was a woman?"

Her partner shook her head and replied, "Looked like a man to me, too."

Butch did have a very masculine appearance and was damn proud of it. She kept her hair short, like a Marine, with only about an inch and a half on top and maybe an inch or less on the sides. Her clothes all came from the Men's department – I'd never once seen her buy anything from the Women's section. Plus, she was never without her baseball cap or chewing tobacco. In many respects I think she considered herself more of a man than a woman; however, she got really pissed if anyone called her a dyke, which, by all lesbian standards, is how she came across.

The four of us waited in the lobby for another thirty minutes before conceding that Shane's family must have snuck by at some earlier point in time. I neglected to tell Michael what I looked like or what I was wearing so he wouldn't have had a clue in identifying me. Assuming they were in the waiting room, I stood in the doorway and scanned the faces of everyone therein, hoping to find someone who looked like Shane. No such luck. Not one person shared her amazing features.

My friends and I claimed an empty group of seats along the back wall and had just sat down when Dr. Brisdale entered the waiting room asking to speak with the family of Shane DuBois. A frail, white-haired woman sitting close to the door rose to her feet at the same time I did.

"I'm her mother," the woman said. "Is my daughter all right?"

A young, handsome man, presumably Shane's brother, took a stand beside her as I moved in behind them.

"She's going to be fine," the doctor answered. "She's suffering from exhaustion and dehydration. I want to keep her here a few days for observation. In her condition, I don't want to take any chances."

"What condition?" her mother asked.

"Miss DuBois is pregnant."

"Pregnant?!?" I shrieked. "That's impossible. There must be some mistake."

"There's no mistake," the doctor chuckled. "Miss DuBois is definitely pregnant. She is already into her second trimester."

"But… We are… I… That's just not possible, doctor. Are you sure?"

Dr. Brisdale laughed again before responding.

"I'm sure. It sounds like you folks need a little time to process this. We should be moving her to her own room within the hour. Someone will be in shortly with the details."

"Thank you," Shane's mother and brother chimed in unison.

"Wow," Biff said softly, leaning over my shoulder. "Pregnant. Go figure."

"Yeah," Marge agreed, leaning in as well. "I never would have guessed that one."

The young man sidestepped Marge and came toward me. With piercing blue eyes, bearded stubble and chiseled, rugged features, he could have easily graced the cover of a GQ magazine. Every woman in the room (all straight, I'm guessing) took notice of him as well, some staring to the point that they had to be prodded by their friends to stop.

"You must be the one who called," he said. "I'm Michael DuBois, Shane's brother. This is our mother, Francis."

I introduced myself again, extending my hand to him and then to his mother. He shook it. She did not.

"Thank you for accompanying my daughter to the hospital," she stated flatly.

"You're wel…"

Cutting me off in mid-sentence, Mrs. DuBois continued.

"You are free to go now. Michael and I will see to it that Shane is taken care of."

"I'd rather stay," I said with an air of authority.

"That won't be necessary."

"I think it *is* necessary, Mrs. DuBois."

"I'm her mother and know what is best for her. You have caused enough trouble."

"Trouble? What trouble have I caused?"

"We both know the answer to that. Shane was fine until you came along."

"Is that right? You surely don't think *I* got her pregnant."

"Don't be absurd."

"I'm not the one who is being absurd."

"This is a family matter. You have no business here."

"That's Shane's decision. Not yours."

"I will not have you upsetting my daughter while she is in this hospital. If I see you anywhere near her room, I will call security and have you escorted out."

Panning my friends' faces, I asked, "Can she do that?"

All three responded by shrugging their shoulders.

"Fine," I grumbled. "Have it your way, lady. I'm outta here!"

I ran from the hospital straight to the parking lot. A frantic search for my car began, and it wasn't until reaching the last row that I remembered riding in the ambulance with Shane. Angrier than ever, I returned to the hospital. Biff was waiting for me outside the lobby doors.

"Get Butch and Marge," I hissed. "I'm ready to go."

"Dusty," she said. Her tone was intentionally calm. "Chill out, okay? Shane's mom just learned that her daughter is in the hospital and that she's pregnant. She doesn't know you and has every right to be concerned. Why don't you try and talk with her again?"

"You can talk to her if you want, Biff. I'm going home."

She reached for my arm but I yanked it away.

"I am not changing my mind," I said. "Are you staying or coming with me?"

"Fine. I'll go get the girls. But I still think you're being unreasonable. You need to talk to Shane and find out what is going on."

"If Shane wants to talk, she knows where to find me."

After collecting the others, we all crammed into Marge's car and drove to a nearby restaurant. No one was particularly hungry so we asked the hostess to forego menus and bring four glasses of water instead. I had barely settled myself down when Biff reiterated that I needed to talk to Shane.

"I heard you the first time," I grumbled.

"Dusty," Marge interjected. "You know I've never been a fan of Shane's, but I have to ask – did she tell you she was pregnant?"

"No, and I don't get it. That's something she should have told me, right? And who the fuck does that mother of hers think she is? She had no right to say that shit to me. What a rude bitch!"

"What are you going to do?" Butch asked.

The first of my tears started to fall as I wailed, "I don't know!"

Laying her hand on my arm, Biff said, "You deserve answers. I don't mean to sound like a broken record but I'll say it again, Dusty. You need to talk to Shane."

"You heard what her mother said. She's not going to let me anywhere near her."

"Don't you worry about that bag of bones," Marge insisted. "I'll make sure the old prune gives you all the time you need. I'll drag her ass out screaming, if I have to."

—— AND BABY MAKES THREE ——

The four of us blazed a path to the hospital and made a beeline for the Information Desk. The attendant told us Shane had been moved to the third floor, so we squeezed into an already full elevator that let us off near the Nurse's Station. Michael was coming out of her room as we approached. As soon as he saw us, he pulled the door closed behind him.

"My mom is in there," he said, crossing his arms and planting himself in the middle of the hallway. It appeared to be an overt attempt to keep us at bay.

"When is she leaving?" Marge asked.

"I'm not sure. Shane is tired so it probably won't be much longer."

He unfolded his arms and took a step toward me. Marge came forward as well, ready and willing to take him out, if necessary. I shooed her back in line behind me.

"It's okay," I assured her. "He wouldn't do anything to me in public."

"Don't be ridiculous," he said in a low voice. It was obvious he didn't want any of the nurses to overhear. "I'm not going to hurt you. I only want to talk to you. You see, I'm not too keen on this woman-to-woman thing you have with my sister. She has never done anything like this before and it has me more than a little concerned."

I wasn't sure if he was making an observation or an accusation, so I remained still and offered no reply. He took another step closer, and, still speaking softly, added, "One thing in your favor is that Shane says she's happy. I love my sister and I want her to be happy. Understand this, though… If you hurt her, I will kill you. Are we clear on that?"

"Crystal," I replied nervously. His words were chilling and I was sure I would wet myself if he continued. Fortunately, he wasn't given the opportunity. At that very moment Mrs. DuBois came out of Shane's room, leaving the door ajar behind her.

"Why are you here?" she fumed. Her eyes, peering at me over the rim of her glasses, never left mine for an instant. "I specifically asked you to stay away."

Standing on tiptoe, I tried to catch a glimpse of Shane but was too short so I turned my full attention to her instead.

"I don't remember you *asking* me anything. I remember you *telling* me to go."

"I will call security if you don't leave. You are not welcome here."

"That isn't up to you. Your daughter is the only one who can make that decision. Until she does, I suggest you butt out."

"You will not speak to me in that fashion, young lady."

"I will speak to you in whatever fashion suits me. Respect is earned, Mrs. DuBois, not simply awarded on the basis of self-perception."

"Mom," Michael said quietly. "I think you should let her by."

His request had no effect. She stood firm, refusing to budge.

"*Mother!*" Shane shouted from her bed.

Mrs. DuBois glanced back at her oldest child.

"Don't make a scene," Shane scolded. "You said you wanted coffee. Why don't you and Michael go down to the cafeteria? I need to talk to Dusty."

"Fine," Mrs. DuBois growled, her beady eyes brimming with disgust. In a tone low enough for only me to hear, she added, "I'm still going to call security."

My friends followed Shane's family into the elevator. Marge wiggled her fingers at me just before the doors closed, which I took as reassurance that Mrs. DuBois was going to be kept on a very short leash. I smiled and gave her a quick wave in return.

I watched the floor indicator change from "3" to "2" before turning back to Shane's room. I lingered in the doorway, a good ten feet or so from her bed.

"How are you?" she asked.

"Stunned, I think. And you?"

She pointed to a chair next to the bed and prompted, "I'd feel better if you weren't so far away. Won't you sit down? It seems we have a lot to talk about."

I ignored the invitation and stood my ground. My teeth were clenched and my jaws flaring as I shoved my hands deep into my pockets.

"Why didn't you tell me you were pregnant, Shane?"

"Because I didn't know."

"How could you not know? There should have been signs. Like morning sickness or missed periods or…"

"I've had screwy periods since I was a teenager. It's not uncommon for me to go three or four months without a cycle. I never gave it a second thought. As for morning sickness, well, it just never happened."

"But how, Shane? When? With who?"

"I'm sure I don't have to tell you *how*, Dusty. The *when* was in mid-January, a few weeks after we… you know, at your office party. I had a business meeting with Giovanni, one of my new Italian importers, to discuss a line of products his company had recently started distributing."

"Doesn't sound like much of a business meeting if you ended up pregnant."

"Let me finish, okay?"

A few seconds passed before she started again.

"I bought several things for the bazaar at that meeting. Giovanni stood to make a hefty commission so he offered to buy cocktails in the hotel bar to celebrate. It was late when we finished and the bar was closing so we moved the party to his room. I guess we let the celebration go too far."

"You think?"

"Look, I was freaked out by what happened between you and me. I've told you that before. I thought maybe sleeping with him would make the memory of that night go away. Anyway, I just assumed he used protection."

"Are you sure he's the father?"

"Yes. Besides you, he's the only person I've been with in the last two years."

"So, what are you going to do?"

"I don't know. I'm scared. Petrified, actually. I wasn't planning on having a baby but the doctor told me I'm too far along for an abortion."

With a trembling hand, she pressed a button on the side rail to elevate her torso.

"I don't want to go through this alone, Dusty. You once told me that you liked kids. What would you think of the two of us raising this child together?"

I looked down and stared at my left foot as it tapped against its mate. Not knowing what to say, I chose to say nothing at all. After an awkward silence, Shane spoke again.

"You barely know me. I get that. You probably want to run from here as fast as possible, right? I know I would."

I glanced in her direction then quickly returned my gaze to my shuffling shoes.

"I don't know, Shane. I'm more than a little weirded out by all of this."

"So am I. Believe me, getting pregnant wasn't in my plans."

I finally looked up and locked eyes with her.

"Maybe you should ask your family for help."

An expression of sadness swept over her face as she turned to look out the window.

"Yeah," she whispered. "Maybe I should."

My mind instantly flooded with a thousand thoughts all at once. *What am I doing?* I protested silently. *This is the woman of my dreams! So, she's pregnant. So what? It isn't like we were seeing each other when it happened. If we were, then I would have good reason to run. But since we weren't...*

A tear rolled down Shane's cheek at the same time a sharp pain pierced my heart. I was convinced it was the Queen Fairy stabbing me with his pitchfork. I moved to stand beside the bed and laid my hand over the rail. Shane quickly covered it with one of her own. I was close to crying as well but shrugged it off, refusing to cave to my emotions in front of her. I needed to stay strong, if not for her benefit, then definitely for my own.

Blinking back a tear, I cleared my throat.

"I'm a better person because of you," I told her. "I can't go back to being who I was before. You are a part of me now and I don't want to lose you."

"Does that mean you'll stay? Is that what you're saying?"

I nodded in agreement then leaned in to kiss her on the cheek. She squeezed my hand and muttered in a quivering voice, "Thank you."

It was becoming harder not to cry, so I took a step back and turned away from her.

"Okay, Shane," I said over my shoulder. "Enough of this mushy stuff. I'm sure your mother wants to see you again before visiting hours are over. I'll go get some of your things and come back later."

I could hear her weeping as I walked toward the door.

"I love you, Dusty," she called out in a tiny, weak voice.

Without turning around, I replied, "I love you, too, Shane."

When I left her room, it felt as though a tremendous weight had been lifted from my shoulders. I rode the elevator down to the first floor and made my way to the cafeteria, anxious to find my friends and share the news with them. My anxiety turned to gratitude as I entered the room and saw three smiling faces waiting to greet me. I looked past them and spotted Mrs. DuBois and Michael at a table in the back. Pointing in their direction, I made a 'talk' gesture with my hand. My friends nodded that they understood.

I slowly approached their table and placed my hands on the back of Mrs. DuBois' chair. Bending slightly at the waist, I brought my face next to hers.

"I'm going to go pick up some things for Shane," I told her. "I'll be back in a couple hours. She's all yours – for now."

Shunning any acknowledgement, Mrs. DuBois rose from her seat and exited the cafeteria. Michael followed in similar fashion. When they were gone, I crossed the room to join my friends.

"How did things go up there?" Marge asked.

"Well, Shane is going to have a baby."

"No shit, Dusty. Tell us something we don't already know."

"We are going to raise it together."

"*What?*" Butch croaked, dumbfounded.

"I want to hear more about this," Biff insisted. "What led to that decision?"

"She said she didn't know she was pregnant and I believe her."

"How could she not know?" Marge asked. "I knew when *I* was pregnant."

"A lifetime of crazy periods and no morning sickness," I countered.

"What about the father?" Biff asked. "Is she planning on telling him?"

"I don't know. She met the guy at a business meeting. They partied a little too much afterwards and had sex. One time – that's all it was."

"Huh," Biff said. "Surely, she's telling the truth. I don't know Shane very well but I don't think she would lie about something as big as this."

"Let's hope not," Marge added.

"This is freaking wild!" Butch exclaimed, her voice shrill with excitement. "Are you sure you're ready for this, Dusty? I mean, you know I'll help in any way I can."

"I will too," Biff added.

"So will I," chimed Marge.

"Thanks, guys. That means a lot. Can you believe it? I'm going to be a parent!"

The three of them took turns, chanting, "And we're going to be aunties!"

- -

Carrying Shane's belongings in a plastic grocery bag, I stepped out of the elevator and walked quietly past the Nurse's Station. The door to her room wasn't completely shut so I pushed it open far enough to slip through. A scruffy looking nurse was standing at the foot of Shane's bed, jotting entries into a chart.

"How is she?" I asked while tiptoeing past her on the balls of my feet.

"She's doing well," the nurse answered without looking up. "Are you family?"

"No. I'm her, uh, friend."

The nurse stopped writing long enough to give me a once over then went right back to her notes.

"Well, 'friend.' You're not supposed to be here. Visiting hours ended thirty minutes ago."

I shook the bag and placed it on the floor beside the chair.

"I'm dropping off some of her things. Is it all right if I stay for a few minutes?"

She lifted her pen from the paper and turned to face me. Her eyes, charcoal like my mother's, gave no indication of humanity behind their dark curtain. Her crude personality was another she-devil trigger for me as well.

"Okay," she said. Her tone sounded rigid, unyielding. "I'm feeling generous so I'll let you stay, but only if you promise not to tell anyone. The Head Nurse is a real Nazi when it comes to enforcing policy around here."

"Thanks," I replied nervously. "And don't worry. Your secret is safe with me."

Her eyes narrowed as she scanned my face, perhaps looking for confirmation that I was telling the truth.

"So, you're just her 'friend,' are you? Miss DuBois mentioned a girlfriend, who I'm guessing would be pretty pissed knowing you're here after hours with her partner."

"All right, detective whatever-your-name-is. I'm the girlfriend."

"Yeah. I clued in on that the moment you snuck in."

Tucking the chart under her arm, she clipped the pen to her lanyard then turned to me once again and smiled. It was a stark contrast to the monster my mind had made her out to be.

"Are you the one who doused this poor woman with chocolate and then had sex with her until she collapsed?"

I immediately felt a spectrum of colors wash over my entire face. The nurse's bushy eyebrows arched and she smiled again, apparently finding humor in my shame.

"Don't be embarrassed, love. Miss DuBois is an attractive woman. If she was my girlfriend, well… Hmmm. There's no good way to finish that sentence. Let's just let her rest, shall we? She needs to recuperate and replenish."

"Yes, ma'am," I answered sheepishly.

"Don't 'ma'am' me," she scoffed. "I am not old enough to be a ma'am yet."

"Sorry. Just being polite."

"Noted. So, 'friend,' what's your name?"

"Dusty. What's yours?"

"The nametag says Andrea, but I prefer Andi."

She latched Shane's chart to the foot of the bed and headed for the door. Before disappearing into the hall, she turned and said, "It was nice meeting you, Dusty. I'm sure I'll see you again on my next rounds."

I waited for her to leave before moving closer to Shane. Her eyes fluttered open as I stooped over to give her a kiss on the forehead.

"Hey there," she mumbled. Her voice sounded parched and tired.

"I brought your pajamas."

"Thank you. I hate these ugly hospital things. Will you help me change?"

Reaching behind her, I untied the laces and, after lifting off her gown, tossed it in the direction of the chair. Andi stuck her head in the door just as I was reaching into the bag for the pajamas. Shane's breasts were fully exposed, giving her quite an eyeful.

"Something told me to come and check on you," she snickered. "You're supposed to let her rest, Dusty. Remember? Shame on you."

"I'm helping her change," I protested. "That's all. Honest!"

"Yeah, right. I'm going on rounds now but will be back soon. Please make sure Miss DuBois is fully clothed when I return."

"Yes, ma'am."

"And don't call me ma'am!" she shouted as the door closed between us.

"Who was that?" Shane asked.

"Your nurse. Her name is Andi."

"You know her?"

"I met her when I came in a little while ago. You were asleep. She's kinda nice, once you get past that crusty exterior."

"What is with her hair?"

"What do you mean?"

"Someone needs to lend her a brush. She looks like she just rolled out of bed."

"Ha! I think that's her style. It seems to fit her, anyway."

"Sounds like you like her."

"Yeah, I think I do."

"Should I be jealous? You can't pick a replacement for me yet. At least wait until I get really big and fat, okay?"

"You're talking crazy, Shane. Now, let's get your top on."

Shane leaned forward while I draped the nightshirt over her shoulders. After her arms were tucked into the sleeves, she pulled the front closed and reclined back against the pillow. While helping her fasten her buttons, my mind flashed back to my office party and the bathroom stall where we first came together.

"Just like that night in December," she said, obviously experiencing the same recall that I was.

I raised my eyes to hers and smiled. Grabbing my shirt, she pulled me forward and kissed me full on the mouth. We were definitely tongue in cheek when Andi peeked in a second time.

"Dusty!" she barked. "Don't make me send you home. I told you she needs rest."

"Don't you have any other patients?" I snarled.

"Yes, I do. However, I feel it is my duty to keep a close eye on this one."

"As you can see, Shane is perfectly fine."

"Good. Keep your hands in your pockets and your mouth above her eyes, got it? I'll be back in fifteen minutes. Good night, ladies."

"Good night," Shane echoed.

After the door closed, Shane said, "I thought you told me she was nice."

We shared a laugh, agreeing it would be best for me to leave before Andi returned. As tired as Shane was, I knew she would be asleep before I made it to the elevator.

As I left the hospital my stomach growled loudly, a not-so-friendly reminder that the only thing I'd eaten all day was the candy offered earlier by my friends. The diner was the only place near my house open twenty-four hours, so I decided to stop in on my way home. While I'd been a frequent patron for many years, now that Shane and I were living together and her love for cooking, there was no real reason to go there anymore.

Mabel, my favorite waitress, greeted me as I came through the door. The diner was empty; no other customers in sight. I ordered a grilled cheese sandwich for takeout and chatted with her until it was ready.

"When did you start working the night shift?" I asked her.

"I'm filling in for Sally Jo. Her son had another asthma attack today."

"Is he okay?"

"I'm sure he'll be fine. I haven't seen you in a while. How are you doing?"

"I'm doing well. Sorry I haven't been by. I'm dating someone and she likes to cook."

"Is this one a keeper?"

"It's looking that way. I'll bring her by sometime so you can meet her."

"I would like that."

"You know, Mabel, this place is starting to look like a dump. When is Joe going to change out those obnoxious tablecloths and paint those nasty walls?"

"You're preaching to the choir, Dusty. I've been here over ten years and we are still using the same gingham covers as when I started. I'll be sure to let the boss know that folks are starting to complain about it, though. Maybe that will light a fire under his ass."

When my order was ready, Benny, the cook, came out of the kitchen and handed me a small Styrofoam container.

"I had a feeling it was you that ordered this," he said. "Here you go. Grilled cheese with extra pickles. Just the way you like it."

When he left, I slipped Mabel a twenty-dollar bill to cover the tab and to give her a generous tip.

"Thanks," I said. "Have a good rest of your night."

"You do the same, Dusty," she responded. "Come back soon!"

Shane slept a good majority of the time she was in the hospital. Andi would stop by during her rounds, providing us an opportunity to become better acquainted. She had a dry sense of humor, like Beth, and some of our conversations had me laughing so hard I thought my sides would split. I truly enjoyed being around her and greatly appreciated the company.

During one of Shane's awake moments, we talked about a nursery for the new baby. Immediately, my imagination kicked in with ideas of what that might look like. I brought a sketchpad on my next visit to keep me occupied while she slept and to fill the quiet hours when there was no one to talk to. On each page I drafted different renditions of the baby's room, then took what I liked most from the drawings and combined them into one sketch. I was just finishing when Shane opened her eyes.

"What are you doing?" she asked after a big, gaping yawn.

"Doodling."

"Can I see?"

"All right. But don't laugh, okay?"

Her eyes lit up when she looked at the picture and she squealed, "Oh my God!"

Andi, who just happened to be walking past the door at that same moment, thought something was amiss and burst into the room.

"Is everything all right?" she asked, hurrying to Shane's bedside.

"Perfect!" Shane answered excitedly.

Seeing that she was okay, Andi breathed a sigh of relief.

Still holding the picture, Shane asked, "Can we hang this in the baby's room?"

Knowing her as I did, her mind was already made up and any attempt to answer wouldn't have mattered so I didn't even bother.

"This is so adorable," she murmured as she continued to stare at the paper.

She showed the drawing to Andi who echoed the same sentiment. Half-grinning, Andi added with a touch of sarcasm, "You're pretty good at that drawing stuff, Dusty. Think you could whip up something for me and sign it? I'd like to get your autograph before you become all famous and full of yourself. Wait… I think I have something you can draw on."

Reaching into her pocket, she pulled out a stick of chewing gum. After shoving the gum into her mouth, she handed me the wrapper.

"Here you go," she announced jokingly. "Draw away, my friend."

"Smart ass," I grumbled jokingly.

She flashed me an impish grin, and, at the same time, Shane did, too.

"I have to get back to work," she said. "Unlike you, Miss DuBois, there are patients in this hospital in dire need of my professional services."

With a twist of her wrist, she vanished into the hall.

Shane giggled, "That girl is something else."

"Yeah, she's something all right," I added in mock agreement.

"I'm glad she was my nurse. It made this whole ordeal more tolerable."

"For both of us."

"Oh… Did I tell you I talked to Mom today? She's still not keen on you and me yet, but she promised to stay out of our affairs and mind her own business."

"Don't force our relationship on her, Shane. If you do, she might end up hating you as much as she hates me."

"She doesn't hate you. She's just being a bitch. I'm going to be happy whether she likes it or not. This is my life, not hers to live through me."

"Do you think she'll ever come around?"

"Eventually. I think we're already making great progress. Didn't she say something to you yesterday?"

"Yeah, 'goodbye.'"

"Well, it's a start."

"I guess."

"I get the impression you'll be as protective of our child as my mom is of me."

"If not more."

Shane shook her head from side to side before muttering, "Lord help us."

Our discussion soon segued into the baby and how he/she was going to drastically alter our lives. Halfway into the conversation, Andi stopped in to let us know that Shane was being discharged the following morning. I jotted my telephone number on the gum wrapper and handed it to her.

"Don't be a stranger," I said. "Keep in touch, okay?"

Andi folded the wrapper and tucked it into her pocket.

"Definitely. I'll give you guys a ring one day next week."

The three of us exchanged hugs and bid each other farewell.

"Do you think she'll really call?" Shane asked after Andi was gone.

"I hope so."

"Me, too. I think she'd be an amazing friend."

—— WE ARE FAMILY ——

Adhering to Dr. Brisdale's orders, Shane spent the next two weeks in bed. Michael suggested she work only part time after that, reminding her that he was totally capable of handling things in her absence. She accepted his offer and pledged to use the extra time to work on the nursery.

Francis stopped by often, at first to visit Shane and then to help her put the baby's room together. Our relationship softened as time passed and we were now at the point where she referred to me by name instead of the "Hey, You" I had grown accustomed to. I called her "Francis" in return, although a few times I slipped and called her "Mom." She didn't seem to mind.

Mother and daughter were always together, working side by side in the nursery from early morning until late at night. One evening I peeked in and saw baby accessories strewn all around the room, just like the ones in my sketch, which was now framed and matted (a gift from Francis, I would later learn) and on display over the crib. Everything seemed to be in its place. All that was missing was the baby.

In June, Shane had her first sonogram and, to my delight, we learned that we were having a girl. It wasn't that I didn't like boys (okay, maybe it was a little), but more that I wanted a mini version of Shane, the most beautiful, kind and generous woman I had ever known. Having two people with those same qualities would have been a blessing.

Francis was there when we were mulling over name choices and suggested "Susan" or "Ann" in honor of Shane's grandmothers. Shane and I wanted something more unique. Our baby wasn't being born into a traditional family, so why give her a traditional name? Neither of us had common names, so it was only fitting we title the baby in similar fashion.

I liked "Alexandra." Shane wanted to call the baby "Dane" because it represented a combination of both our names. After switching the order several times, we finally settled on "Dane Alexandra DuBois." Francis loved it. Michael approved as well, claiming it had a nice, rhythmic flow to it. Our friends endorsed the choice, too, and so it became official.

Shane was about to enter her eighth month of pregnancy and we were standing in the nursery one day having a discussion about formula, bottles, diaper pails and onesies when, all of a sudden, out of the blue, she announced that she wanted to have a party.

"A party?" I repeated. "For what?"

"Not for *what*, silly. For *whom*. For Dane!"

"You mean like a baby shower?"

"Yeah. Doesn't that sound fun?"

"I wouldn't know. I've never been to one. Do lesbians even have baby showers?"

"Lesbians have babies, don't they? Why wouldn't they have baby showers?"

"Huh. I guess that makes sense."

"What about week after next? It's kind of quick but I think we can pull it off. You can design the invitation and I will personally hand deliver them since I'm still only going to the store on a part time basis."

Patting her round belly, she smiled and a radiant glow came over her face.

"Dane's awake. Hurry, come put your hand on my stomach."

My hand was barely atop her bellybutton before it was kicked away by one of the baby's extremities.

"I think she wants out," I chuckled.

Shane draped her arms over my shoulders and started nuzzling on my earlobe, a tactic she often used to get to me to do something menial. I'm not sure if it was because I was gullible or whipped (or both), but it always seemed to work in her favor.

"I'm hungry," she whispered in my ear.

No big surprise there. 'Hungry' was her usual condition of late. Since moving in, she made sure there was never a shortage of food. And, if anything was stale or outdated, it got thrown away. Post haste.

Her ploy worked as intended and I was volunteered to whip up some snacks for the expectant mother. She stayed behind in the nursery while I went in search of something for her to eat. Satisfying her cravings over the course of her pregnancy had been quite the challenge, but less so in the last couple of weeks. Knowing it wouldn't matter what I chose, I decided to make something *I* wanted instead. After checking out what was in the pantry, I took out a bag of tortilla chips, poured them into a large bowl and had just opened the refrigerator to retrieve a jar of salsa when the phone rang. Thinking she would answer it, I continued with my task. After several rings I realized I had missed the mark with that assumption, so I rushed back to the nursery and snatched the telephone from the table beside the rocking chair, which Shane was sitting in. Glaring at her, I placed the receiver next to my ear.

"What?" she challenged in her now perfected princess mode. "I thought *you* were going to answer it."

Still giving her the evil eye, I shouted into the receiver, "Hello!"

"Wow," a woman's voice bellowed back. "Ain't that a fine howdy-do."

I smiled, my visual venting at Shane quickly subsiding as I recognized Andi's voice.

"Hey, chick. What's shakin'?"

"Nothing but my flabby arms, girl. How are ya? And how's the fat lady doing?"

"Great. We're both great. How are you?"

"I'm peachy. I just wanted to call and say hi and see what y'all were up to."

"Actually, we were just talking about having a baby shower."

"Isn't it a bit early for that? She's only about six and half months now, right?"

"No. She'll be eight months next week!"

"I stand corrected. So, when is the big event?"

"Week after next. Think you can you make it?"

"If I'm not working, I'll be there with bells on."

"Bells are kinda loud, Andi. How about something quieter?"

"You are such a dud, Dusty."

"I know. Shane likes me that way."

"Thank goodness someone does."

"Back to the party... Shane is personally delivering the invitations and we need your address. I'm designing them myself."

"Another work of art? Since I never got your autograph at the hospital, would you be a doll and sign one of those for me?"

"Whatever. I hope we'll see you at the party!"

I handed the phone to Shane to get Andi's address and went over instructions with her on what she should do if it were to ring again. She tossed her head back and laughed, then quickly reached out and pinched my nipple. I yelped and made a dash for the door.

I returned to the kitchen and finished pouring the salsa then situated both bowls in the crook of one arm, grabbed my sketchpad from the living room and returned to the nursery. After handing the snacks to Shane, I sat cross-legged on the floor in front of her and spread the tablet open across my lap.

I began to giggle as my thoughts came to life on paper – a caricature of Shane with an exaggerated, oversized stomach, her hands clasped tightly together below her bulging belly. In the drawing I am standing behind her, my hands cupped over hers as we struggle together to hold up the excess load. I titled the invitation, *"HURRY!"*

My giggle quickly morphed into a snort-filled, pee-in-your-pants kind of hilarity. Shane, whose only interest up to this point was food, leaned forward to ask what was so funny. I raised the sketch for her to see and she began to laugh as well.

"What in the world?"

"It's our invitation. Isn't it funny?"

"Hilarious! I love it! Now go get the calendar so we can pick a date."

"Why don't you go get the calendar?"

"Because I'm pregnant."

"That's your excuse for everything. It won't work this time, sister. And don't even think about messing with my earlobes, either. I am onto you and your sinister ploys. I'm going to stay right here and enjoy the chips and salsa while *you* go get the calendar."

"Damn," she huffed, her smile turning into a pout then back to a grin. "All this time I thought I was getting away with something."

I continued eating chips the entire time she was away, dunking them so far into the salsa that my fingers looked like they were bleeding tomatoes. She returned not long after with the calendar, a pickle and a banana.

"Ewww," I said, grimacing. "What a disgusting combination."

"It wasn't my choice, believe me. This is all your daughter's doing."

Waving the pickle and banana in front of my face, she teased, "Dane wants you to share these yummy things with us."

"Tell her thanks but I'm perfectly content with the chips and salsa."

"Hold this stuff for me while I get situated, okay?"

Before I could answer she shoved the pickle in my mouth and dropped the banana onto my sketchpad. After settling back into the rocker, she flipped open the calendar to the month of September and reclaimed the pickle.

"What about the thirteenth?" she asked between bites. "It's a week from Friday."

"Friday the thirteenth? Isn't that bad luck?"

"I didn't know you were superstitious. I'm not. I say we go for it!"

I turned to face her, the pungent aroma of dill permeating the air between us.

"Whatever you want, dear. It's your party."

Crunching loudly, she muttered, "I told you the party isn't for me. It's for Dane."

She then motioned for me to pass her the banana. After peeling the outer skin back, she bit off a mouthful then snatched the pen from my hand. She drew a circle around the date on the calendar and scribbled "DANE'S PARTY" in the white space below.

"This is going to be so much fun," she said as she leaned forward to kiss the top of my head. Her bloated tummy caused her to fall short so she put her hands under my chin and started tugging on my head to close the gap.

"Ouch, Shane! You're pulling my head off!"

"Sorry! I'm just so excited about this party, Dusty! I can't wait!"

Laying the tablet aside, I turned around and rose up onto my knees to share a real kiss with her, face to face. Her enthusiasm was more than enough for the both of us and I couldn't help but smile in return.

- -

I left work early the day before the shower to pick up one last present. I had already visited most of the baby stores in Dallas the previous week and purchased practically every newborn item I came in contact with. My trunk was packed full of things for Dane (hidden there so Shane wouldn't find them), and, sifting through it all, it was obvious that our little girl was going to be the cleanest, driest, best dressed and prettiest smelling child in all of Texas. And, judging by the look of things, she was going to have more toys than any other kid in the state as well.

The baby gifts still needed to be wrapped, but there would be time enough for that tomorrow. Today was all about Shane in that I was buying two gifts for her as well. One, a breast pump (yuck) that she had asked for, was tucked under my front seat. The other, a diamond ring, was at the jewelers for sizing. The advantage of sharing living expenses with her made it possible for me to stash away a few bucks here and there and I had finally saved up enough to buy the tiniest rock in the store, knowing full well I would replace it with a larger stone as soon as I could afford to.

I'd been mulling over the idea of proposing for weeks but hadn't decided on a good time to actually pop the question. When Shane suggested the baby shower, the answer fell into my lap (literally, at the same time as the banana). I knew it would serve as the perfect cover. I told no one about it. Not even my friends knew of my intentions.

The morning of the party, I hinted to Shane that she was getting a big surprise that night. She tried everything, including sexual enticement, to get me to spill, but I resisted. She must have thought I would give in if she let me have my way with her but, even after making love, I still refused to divulge any details. Not getting the outcome she was hoping for, she stormed into the bathroom, slamming the door behind her.

"Be mad if you want," I yelled after her. "It won't change anything. You have to wait until tonight to get your surprise."

The door swung open and she emerged, still naked, with her arms folded together over the top of her stomach.

"Come on, Dusty," she pleaded. "If you really loved me, you would tell me what the surprise is."

"Give it up, Shane. You'll find out at the party with everyone else."

"You haven't told anyone? Not even Biff? Or Butch?"

"Butch? Are you kidding? She's worse than Marge at keeping secrets. I haven't told anyone because I want them to be surprised as well. I hate to bust your bubble, but I am the only one who knows."

"Fine," she snapped, storming back into the bathroom. The door slammed behind her once more.

Not knowing how long she would stay mad I chose to ignore her tantrums and get on with my day. There were pre-party errands to run and I needed to get a move on. As I was rummaging through my drawers for something to wear, she came up behind me and tapped me on the shoulder.

"Give me a clue," she grumbled. "Will you? Something. Anything."

"No. For the last time, I'm not telling."

"I had no idea you could be so cruel."

"I'm sorry you think I'm being mean. You won't think that way after tonight."

I puckered my lips for a smooch but she brushed me off instead.

"The only kiss you'll get from me will be in your dreams," she hissed.

"You're so spoiled. Did your mom give in to this behavior when you were a kid?"

"Yes, she did."

"Then you need to take a closer look, honey. I ain't your mama. But while we're on the subject, why don't you go hang out with Francis for a couple of hours?"

"Are you trying to get rid of me?"

"I have lots to do before the party. Go on now. I really want this to be a surprise."

"The surprise had better be worth all of this, Dusty."

"It will be. I promise."

We finished dressing in silence and arrived at the front door together. I leaned in for another kiss but she snubbed me again. She did, however, allow me a kiss on her belly for Dane.

"When can I come home?" she asked in a huff.

"Not before six. Go out and have some fun with your mom, okay? I love you."

"If you really loved me…"

"Yeah, yeah. You know I love you, Shane. And in a few hours, you'll be more in love with me than ever."

I walked her to her car and opened the door, then quickly trotted over to my own vehicle and sped away. The jeweler was the first stop on my agenda, followed by the party store and then the bakery at the neighborhood market.

I arrived home at 2:45 after collecting the ring and party favors, which gave me just enough time to unload the car and gulp down a can of pop before heading to the market. At 4:00 I returned with the cake and set it on the counter, then filled a glass with ice water and plopped down at the table. The glass had barely reached my lips when the phone rang.

"Party Central!" I sang into the receiver.

"Dusty, this is Andi."

"Hey, girl. What are you up to? You aren't calling to cancel, are you?"

"No, I'm not calling about that. Listen, there's been an accident. Shane is at the hospital. You need to get down here right away."

"Is she all right?" I asked, rising from my chair.

"Just hurry, Dusty."

I hung up and immediately called Butch, my fingers trembling uncontrollably as they came in contact with the keypad. A wave of nausea knocked me back into my seat as I repeated Andi's message. I then asked her to relay the news to Marge and Biff.

"Of course I will," she said. "Call as soon as you know what's going on with Shane."

- -

The hospital was a little more than fifteen minutes from my house but I made it in ten. Hurrying in from the parking lot, I found Andi outside of the Emergency Room doors.

"Dusty," she whispered nervously, reaching for my hand. "Come with me."

"What is it, Andi? Where's Shane?"

She said nothing as she led me into an office and closed the door behind us.

"Sit down," she said, then quickly added, "God, I wish I didn't have to tell you this."

"Tell me what, Andi?"

"Shane was in a terrible accident, sweetie. She was hit head on by a drunk driver a few hours ago. An ambulance just happened to be nearby and the paramedics brought her here to the hospital. The doctors did all that they could but her injuries were too severe. They weren't able to save her. I've left a ton of messages for you. Where were you?"

"Picking up stuff for the baby shower."

"Oh my God. That was tonight?"

Looking her squarely in the face, I nodded. Tears began pooling in her eyes. She let out a deep breath, lowered her head and continued.

"There were urgent decisions to be made, so the hospital called Shane's mother. As soon as she arrived, she gave the authorization to perform a cesarean and to…"

She raised her hand and placed it over her mouth in an unsuccessful attempt to silence her cries. Tears were now spilling over onto her cheeks.

"And to… *What*?" I screamed. My heart was racing, pounding against my temples and resonating in my eardrums.

"…to remove her from life support."

"Where is she? Where is Shane?"

"She's in the morgue, honey. If you want, I'll take you to her."

I followed her through a maze of corridors into a part of the hospital I never knew existed. We stopped outside of a large, open room where I could see Shane lying on a table with a sheet draped over her through a small window on the door. Andi took my hand and led me inside.

"I'm so sorry," I heard her say as I passed in front of her.

I inched my way toward Shane. When I finally reached the table, I leaned forward and stroked the side of her face.

"She's cold," I said to no one in particular. Turning to Andi, I repeated, "She's cold. Can you get her a blanket?"

"She doesn't need a blanket, Dusty. She's already gone."

Her words pierced my very core. Overwhelmed with emotion, I backed away and shoved my hands into my pockets. There, alongside a handful of change, was the jeweler's box. I lifted the ring from its case and held it before Shane's closed eyes.

"Look!" I shouted. "Here is your damn surprise! All morning you begged me to tell you but I wouldn't. If I had, maybe this wouldn't have happened. This is all my fault!"

Andi took a step toward me and stopped. "This wasn't your fault," she proclaimed in a hushed voice. "It was an accident."

I ignored her, choosing instead to continue my conversation with Shane.

"You told me I didn't have to be afraid anymore. Well, I'm very afraid right now. Come on, Shane. Get up, okay? Please? Don't do this, damn it! Don't leave me!"

"Dusty," Andi said. "There's somewhere else you need to be."

"I can't leave her here all alone, Andi."

"That isn't her, honey. Shane's not with us anymore. She's gone."

"She can't be gone. I was going to propose to her tonight. At the shower. See? Look! Here's the ring!"

I held the diamond band in the air for her to see. Then, in a moment of rage, I threw the empty box in her direction. She caught it just before it hit the floor.

"I'm sorry, Dusty. If it was in my power, I would bring her back for you. It's too late for Shane, but it's not too late for your baby."

Rage consumed me as my eyes scanned Shane's lifeless body. I clenched my fingers tightly around the ring then opened my hand and let it fall to the floor. Andi slipped her arm around my waist and steered me toward the door.

"Come on, Dusty," she urged. "Let me take you to see your daughter."

Outside of the room, I turned and pressed my forehead against the window for one last look at Shane.

"Why did this happen, Andi?"

"I don't know, sweetie. No one knows why stuff like this happens."

"Where's Francis?"

"With the baby."

"Is Dane okay?"

"They're running tests to see if she suffered any injuries in the accident. The next few days will be critical. She needs you, honey. She needs your strength to pull through."

"I don't have anything left to give her."

Pointing to my heart, Andi said, "Yes you do. Everything you need is in there."

- - - - - - - - - - - - - - - - - -

We passed through another labyrinth of corridors before arriving at the Neonatal Intensive Care Unit. The door opened and I saw Francis and Michael holding hands and staring down into an incubator.

"Is that her?" I asked Andi. "Is that Dane?"

"Yes, Dusty. That's her. Go on over and say hello to your little girl." She draped her arm over my shoulder and gave me a gentle squeeze.

"Go on," she repeated, nudging me toward the incubator. "Be with your family. I'll wait for your friends downstairs."

Michael put his hand on my back and ushered me in between him and Francis. The three of us stood shoulder to shoulder staring at that tiny little baby in the long glass tube. I slid my hand into the gloved insert and reached inside. Dane's fingers instantly latched onto mine and her head turned in my direction as if she were expecting me. The rush of emotions when I looked into her bright, blue eyes was overwhelming.

"Hello, Dane," I said. "I'm Dusty. I'm so very happy to finally meet you. I see you've already met your grandmother and your uncle. Don't be afraid, little one. You are not alone. We are right here with you."

"Don't give up," Michael urged. "Be a fighter like your mama, you hear?"

"She looks like Shane," Francis whispered. Her words sounded frail and defeated.

"Yes, she does," I agreed.

"She's so small," Michael added. "She barely takes up any space in there."

Dane squeezed my fingers again then released as the machines around her began sounding an alarm. A nurse rushed over and shoved us aside.

"What's going on?" Michael asked.

"Please step out of the room," the nurse said flatly.

"Why?" I asked nervously. "What is happening?"

"Please," the nurse repeated. "We need to get her stabilized."

Francis, Michael and I moved to the hall and remained huddled together until Andi arrived with my friends. Marge and Biff approached Francis and hugged her, both offering their sincerest, heartfelt condolences. Butch came to stand next to me.

"Are you okay?" she asked.

I shook my head slowly from side to side.

"How's the baby?" Biff asked.

"We don't know yet," Michael told her. "The machines she was hooked up to started going off so they told us to wait out here."

"There's a waiting room near the elevator," Marge said. "Maybe we should all go in there instead of standing out here in the hall."

"Good idea," Andi agreed. "I'll let the nurse know where to find you."

As we turned to go, a tall man in green hospital scrubs came toward us.

"Are you related to baby DuBois?" he asked, stopping in front of Francis.

Francis squeezed my hand before answering.

"Yes. She is my granddaughter."

"I'm sorry," he expressed with remorse as he gently laid his hand on her shoulder. "We couldn't save her. I hate to ask this right now, but we need a name to assign to the death certificate."

Shock kept Francis from answering so Michael spoke instead.

"Dane," he stated proudly. "Her name is Dane Alexandra DuBois."

Francis' grip on my hand loosened and I was sure she was going to faint. Bringing my face close to hers, I whispered, "Go home, Francis."

"I can't," she answered back. "I need to stay and make the arrangements."

"Dusty is right," Michael argued. "This is too much for you to deal with right now. I can take care of everything here."

Panning the sad faces of my friends, I asked, "Could one of you drive her home and stay with her until Michael gets there?"

"I will," Marge volunteered.

"Thank you," Francis said. "My daughter thought so highly of each and every one of you. Now I know why. I'm sorry I ever thought otherwise."

Returning to my side, Butch put her arm around my waist.

"I can stay if you want me to," she said.

Biff chimed in, "I can stay, too."

"I appreciate the offer, but no thanks. This is a lot to process and I..."

My words trailed off as I struggled to collect my thoughts and harness my emotions at the same time. Moments later, I mumbled, "I'll call you guys later."

Biff was insistent that I not be left alone and challenged, "Are you sure?"

"Yeah, I'm sure."

The five females walked to the elevator together while Michael and I trailed behind them. It was a relatively short distance from where we were standing, but it seemed like the longest journey of my life.

Francis and I shared a long embrace that ended in a sad, tearful goodbye. A flurry of hugs and kisses were then exchanged between all members of our group. After they left, Michael stooped over and placed his hands on his knees.

"I'm not sure I can do this," he said, sniffling several times after he spoke.

Andi rubbed his back and told him, "I'm here for you." Turning to me, she added, "For both of you."

- -

Andi cleared it with the nurse for Michael and I to see Dane one more time. Michael went first, and, when he came out, his eyes were red and swollen. The shock of everything he had experienced that day was apparent as his face remained expressionless.

And then it was my turn.

"Take as long as you'd like," the nurse told me.

The incubator lid was open so I laid one hand on Dane's stomach and stroked the side of her face with the other.

"You were taken away before I got the chance to know you, my sweet, little girl. For that, I am truly sorry. But you weren't taken away before I got the chance to love you. And for that, I am truly blessed."

My tears were pooling on Dane's chest. I lost my composure at that point and had to clear my throat before continuing.

"I promise to never forget you, my love. Please don't ever forget me."

Transferring my hands to my own face, I wept openly. Then, from somewhere deep within, a soulful wail passed through my body and pierced the stillness. Michael rushed into the room and held out his arms to me. I collapsed against his chest.

"What am I going to do?" I sobbed. "Where do I go from here?"

"Wherever that is, know that you won't be alone," he pledged. I could feel his chest rumbling as he spoke. "Me, Andi, your friends...

We'll always be there for you." Chuckling, he added, "Heck, you've even got my mother now, too, whether you wanted her or not!"

I peered into his eyes and saw the slightest hint of a smile trapped behind his pain. That expression faded quickly as he dropped his arms and turned away from me.

"I'm so goddamn angry," he shouted out loudly, then lowered his voice to continue, "Two innocent lives were taken by an idiot who chose to drink and drive. Who does that? Who gets drunk in the middle of the day? It's a good thing that son of a bitch died in the crash or I would have snuffed the life out of him with my bare hands."

He turned back to face me and once again took me into his arms.

"My sister loved you very much," he confided, tightening his grip as he spoke. "Her entire world changed the day she met you. Did you know that? She wanted nothing more than for the two of you to have a long and fantastic life together."

"That's all gone now, Michael," I cried into his shirt. "Even a future with Dane. All gone. Maybe I wasn't meant to be loved. Maybe being alone and miserable is how my life was supposed to turn out."

"Don't say that, Dusty. I truly believe that Shane was brought into your life to show you that you *are* worthy of being loved."

"So, what am I supposed to feel now, Michael? Happy? Grateful?"

"Yes. Happy that someone as beautiful as Shane wanted to share her life with you. Grateful that she loved you unconditionally. You were loved – that is what you take away from this. She loved you enough to share her child with you – that is what you take away from this. My sister told me that you were dealt a shitty hand as a kid, Dusty, but everyone deserves to be loved and my sister loved you without limits – that is what you take away from this."

He waved for Andi to join us and then asked to speak with her privately. She agreed and they moved a few steps away. Though they spoke quietly, I still could hear every word of their conversation.

"This may sound strange," Michael told her, "and it may not be protocol, but I know my sister would want to be with her baby. Can you make that happen?"

"No problem," Andi answered. "Wait for me in the lobby and I'll come get you when everything is taken care of."

We rode the elevator down to the first floor together, Michael's big hand clutching mine for the better part of the ride. Nearly an hour passed before we saw Andi again.

"It's done," she announced as she approached us.

—— GOODBYE TO LOVE ——

Michael and I followed Andi to the same room she had taken me when I arrived at the hospital. Standing in the hall, I took a deep breath and let it out slowly. I thought that Michael and I would go in together, but, as I reached for the door, he stopped me and said in a trembling voice, "I'd like to go in first if that's okay with you, Dusty. By myself."

I took his hand in mine and smiled.

"I've only known Shane a few months, Michael. You've known her your entire life. It's only fitting that you go first."

His bottom lip was quivering and a flurry of tears were streaming down his cheeks as he squeezed my hand and whispered in response, "Thank you."

My heart ached for him – and for Shane, who would never again tell stories about her magnificent little brother. My heart ached for Dane as well, as she would never have the opportunity of growing up with such a wonderful man in her life. Instantly, my mind filled with flashes of Dane at milestones we all should have witnessed in her life: first day of school, prom, graduation. Each image was like a knife plunging straight into my heart.

I knew Shane loved me. I was sure of that. She had told me on so many occasions. But the baby – *my* baby – well, there just hadn't been enough time. I'm sure Dane sensed the love I had for her. When she squeezed my finger, I believed she was letting me know that she loved me, too.

My turn came and I entered the room slowly, anchoring my feet inside the door for what seemed like an eternity. I finally mustered the courage and moved toward the table. Caressing both of their faces, I kissed Shane first and then Dane, wetting their cheeks with my tears as I said my final goodbyes.

It was midnight when we left the hospital. Michael offered to walk Andi and me to our cars and we graciously accepted. Along the way, he asked if he could stop in to see the nursery before going to his mother's house. Francis and Shane had raved on and on about it, he said, and he wanted to see for himself what all the fuss was about. I'm sure he had other reasons as well, but I didn't pry.

When we arrived at my house, I directed him to the nursery then headed off to start a pot of coffee. Painful reminders of how my evening was supposed to unfold practically floored me as I entered the kitchen and saw the cake box and party decorations on the counter. It was too much to bear and I ran down the hallway, slamming Michael into a wall along the way.

"What is it, Dusty?" he called out after me. "What's wrong?"

Hurrying past him, I went straight to the nursery. The teddy bear Shane had been holding the night before was still in the rocking chair, just where she had left it. I picked it up and pressed it tightly against my chest as I lowered myself into the seat. Emptiness enveloped me and I soon became numb to its effect.

- -

On September 20, 1996, Shane and Dane were buried in a shared casket. Dane was nestled in her mother's arm with her head tucked against Shane's chin. Francis' tailor had created matching outfits for them, both mother and infant beautifully paired in light blue dresses with a hummingbird, Shane's favorite, embroidered into their white bodices.

Michael started to read the eulogy but his eyes quickly filled with tears and he had to stop to blot them away with the back of his coat sleeve. Biff handed him a box of tissues and, after wiping his eyes, he blew his nose and apologized then shoved the tissue into his pocket and started again, this time finishing with only an occasional pause to recompose. Francis wanted to speak as well but fell apart at the podium and had to be helped back to her seat. I knew I wouldn't make it through the first word, so I didn't even try.

At the gravesite everyone was given a red rose to place on the casket before it was lowered into the ground. The number of roses quickly multiplied as friends and family all came forward to bid their final farewells.

Francis, Michael and I clung tightly to one another as we stood beside the floral-laden coffin. I kissed my rose and gently laid it on top of the others; Francis and Michael did the same. My friends and coworkers, as well as a long parade of supporters who knew Shane then passed before us, each one sharing their deepest sympathies.

— — — — — — — — — — — — — — — — — —

With Shane gone, taking my meals at the diner had once again become part of my routine. I knew that the diner was running a special on Thanksgiving dishes that week, so I decided to stop in for lunch before going to the cemetery. Mabel, as usual, greeted me at the door and ushered me to my booth. Once I sat down, however, the smells weren't so appealing and I decided to go with my usual instead.

"I don't know why I even bother with this," she said as she handed me a menu. "I know you won't look at it."

"Not today, Mabel. Maybe I will tomorrow."

"You always say that, Dusty. Tomorrow is never going to come for you."

"You're probably right."

"Grilled cheese? Same as always?"

I smiled and nodded. Looking around, I could see that nothing about the place had changed. The walls were more in need of a fresh coat of paint than ever while the same old, tattered gingham cloths still topped every table.

"Wasn't Joe supposed to start renovations last week?" I asked.

"Yeah. I guess he decided to put it off again."

"It might bring in more customers if he spiffed things up a bit."

"I'm sure it would. Business is always slow around this time of year so I doubt he'll do anything until next year."

"It's slow at the print shop, too. I might take some time off for a few days."

"I think you should. You've been looking pretty tired lately. More so each time you come in here. Maybe you should skip the sandwich and go home and rest."

"Not a bad idea, but I'm too hungry."

"How about a bowl of tomato soup with your sandwich today?"

"Sure. That sounds good."

"Tea or Pepsi with that?"

"I'll have a Pepsi. Thanks."

After she left, I tapped a cigarette out of the pack and followed that with my lighter. My first drag was a long one and I let it trickle out slowly afterwards. Smoke haloed above my head like a dense haze shrouding fields of grass on a cool autumn morning.

"Did you go to the cemetery today?" Mabel asked when she returned with my drink.

"Not yet. I plan to go by there on my way home."

"I wish I could have met Shane."

"You would have like her."

"I really am sorry for your loss, Dusty. You know I'm here if you ever want to talk."

"I appreciate that, Mabel."

I finished my lunch and then collected my things to leave. Living on my own again, I was back on a budget and couldn't afford to splurge on a big tip, so, I left a ten and two ones to cover the bill and have a little something left over for Mabel.

My frequent trips to the cemetery had become so familiar that I made the drive without much conscious thought anymore. On that day, though, I purposely took my time getting there, taking time to view the beautiful fall colors along the way.

I pulled into a parking spot and shut off the engine then grabbed my jacket and got out of the car. Looking ahead I couldn't make out Shane's headstone, but the landscaping crew was onsite and there was so much grass and leaves on the ground that it didn't create any immediate cause for concern. When the marker didn't materialize as I came closer, my first thought was that vandals must have taken it.

That's ludicrous, I reassured myself. *Why would anyone steal a headstone?*

I arrived at the location I had been visiting at least twice a week since the funeral, but instead of standing next to Shane's grave I found myself on an undisturbed patch of land. I turned in a full circle, twisting my head slightly in each direction for confirmation that I was in the right place. Nothing, except for the very spot where I stood, seemed out of the ordinary. Everything else looked exactly as it had the last time I was there.

I turned and scanned the horizon again. To my right was the same tree that served as my landmark since first coming to the cemetery, standing tall at the intersection closest to Shane's grave. The concrete bench was still there as well. Tips of red rose petals were poking out from under a pile of leaves on the plot next to Shane's, remnants of the bouquet Mrs. Jones' son had left there in honor of her 80th birthday.

What the hell is going on? I wondered. *I was here two days ago when he put those flowers out for her...*

My confusion heightened; I began to panic. I quickly left the cemetery and raced back to the diner.

"Is Mabel here?" I asked the hostess as I rushed inside.

"I believe she's in the kitchen," she replied. "Or at least she was a few minutes ago. Is something wrong?"

I ignored her and ran toward the rear of the restaurant.

"Mabel!" I shouted. "Mabel!"

Mabel emerged from the kitchen with an armful of plates. Sensing my urgency, she set them down and came right over.

"What in the world is the matter, Dusty? Are you okay?"

"You knew where I was going when I left here, right?"

"Yes. You said you were going to the cemetery."

"She wasn't there."

"What?"

"Shane! She wasn't there!"

"What in the world are you talking about? How can that be?"

"I don't know."

"Well, for heaven's sake. I don't understand…"

I suddenly recalled my last daydream and asked her, "What day is it, Mabel?"

"Excuse me?"

"What day is it?"

"It's Sunday."

"No. What *date* is it?"

"November 17th. Why?"

"What year?"

"Huh?"

"Tell me what goddamn year it is!"

"It's 1995."

"Wait a minute… Shane didn't die until 1996!"

—— THE GIRL OF MY DREAMS ——

It had definitely been a night filled with tossing and turning. Exhausted, I managed to crawl out of bed and make it to work on time. It turned out to be an excruciatingly slow workday, unusual for the week leading up to Thanksgiving. Beth and Maggie and I were standing around with nothing to do, so we decided to pass the time tidying up around the production area. Afterwards, we started gossiping and I was about to launch into a new lesbian tale when a particularly striking woman entered the store. A feeling of déjà vu nearly knocked my feet out from under me as she approached the counter.

"Dusty," Beth said in a low voice. "You're white as a ghost. Are you okay?"

"Have you ever dreamed about something before it happened?" I asked.

"Yeah. I think everyone has. Why?"

"I've seen that woman in my dreams."

"I'm sure you have, Dusty. She's very attractive."

Maggie smiled at the fair-skinned beauty and asked, "Can I help you?"

Large dimples appeared as the women smiled in return. My heart suddenly began to beat erratically and my knees felt like they were going to buckle under my weight as she came toward us.

"Hello," the woman said. "I'm here to pick up my order. I believe all of those boxes in the corner are mine. Could one of you help me carry them to my car?"